CHALLENGER STORM
THE ISLE OF BLOOD

AIRSHIP 27 PRODUCTIONS

CHALLENGER STORM-ISLE OF BLOOD
© 2011 Don Gates

Published by Airship 27 Productions
www.airship27.com www.airship27hangar.com

Interior & cover illustrations © 2011 Michael W. Kaluta

Editor: Ron Fortier
Associate Editor: John Bruening
Production and design by Rob Davis
Promotions Manager: Michael Vance

First Airship 27 Productions edition

ISBN-13: 978-0692340783 (Airship 27)
ISBN-10: 0692340785

Printed in the United States of America

10 9 8 7 6 5 4 3 2 1

Acknowledgements

Dedicated to my hero: my late father, Detective Don Gates, Jr. I miss and love you very much. To my mother, who never said "no" when I wanted a new book. To Ron, Rob, and Michael K.: thank you for putting it all together. To my team of "feedback scientists" Luis Gabriel Leal, Manny DeJesus (inventor of the acid-bolo), Dave Flora (designer of the MARDL wing & wrench logo), Tom Floyd, and Michael B.: a million thanks for helping me to sharpen the point on this thing. To Doc Ferus, Matthew "The Wolf" and all the readers of my blog and Storm fans on Myspace and Facebook: thank you for your interest and your belief in me. To Chuck: thanks for being my friend. And to my beautiful and angelic wife, Annie, without whom I wouldn't be typing these words: thank you for loving me through it all and for being who you are... you truly make miracles happen.

PROLOGUE...

Che sky was bloated with deep grey clouds; among them stitched angry flashes of lightning, and the whole sky seemed to be holding its breath, waiting.

The heavily modified tri-motored airplane shimmied in the buffeting wind, but otherwise was kept steady under the guidance of the man behind the controls. He was a young man in his early twenties, his pomaded blonde hair slicked back and shiny in the dim light of the cockpit. Nervously, he chewed his lip as he studied the dark clouds.

"I don't like this, boss. We should go around this storm." Lightning slashed by the plane and he winced. "We could get cooked up here. How can we stop these guys if we're dead?"

"That's what they're counting on, Skids… that we won't follow them," a voice called back from the rear of the plane. "They're crazy for trying to follow the storm, but they're counting on no one else being crazy, too."

"Well, I still think you might be a few cards short of a deck, Cliff," said a deeper voice further back in the plane. "What you're trying to do is suicide."

"I'll be okay. Even though the winch hasn't been tested yet, the boys in the lab say it should be okay. Trust me. Everything will be alright."

"Yeah, pipe down and let him kill himself, Brock," the pilot said.

"Can it, squirt," boomed the deep voice coming closer now to the cockpit.

"Both of you, knock it off," said the third man with a chuckle as he entered the front of the plane. He leaned over and scrutinized the sky ahead of the windscreen. His tone turned serious. "I need to concentrate. We should be catching up with them soon."

The eyes that looked out across the torrid sea of slate-colored clouds were blue-grey and somehow old, even though they were set in a young face. The face was calm in demeanor, and could be considered handsome apart from the three deep scars that marred the left side of his face. The longest of these extended from the dark hair at his temple all the way down his face and throat, disappearing into the collar of the jumpsuit he wore. He was built like a marathon runner; his physique was not huge but was well-developed and toned. There was a tense energy that seemed to radiate from Clifton Storm, like a wound-up spring waiting for action, and he drummed his fingers on the instrument panel before him.

A few minutes went by and the sky remained empty of all but the plane and the raging tempest. It had started to rain and apart from the thunder, the pattering of droplets against the tin hull and the drone of the plane's engines, the miles ticked by in silence.

The third man entered the cockpit, a looming and muscular mountain. He was bald and mustached, and his arms were thickly covered with tattoos. He stood beside the scarred man and looked out across the sky.

"The damned thing's called Goliath, so you'd think it'd be pretty easy to see...so where is it?" asked the big man named Brock. He crossed his thick arms impatiently, their tattoos rippling. "You think they got away?"

As if on cue, a gigantic silver shape slowly rose out of the clouds ahead of them. Like the back of a rising monstrous breaching whale, the enormous dirigible broke above a thick black cloud-bank. The Goliath had a unique double-gasbag design, and it was covered with an extensive framework of open girders. A breathtaking mixture of ugly industrial utility and gracefully streamlined airship, the huge craft dwarfed the tri-motor, and the three men inside were stunned into silence.

"Geez..." Skids finally breathed. It sounded small and childlike in the cockpit.

After a few moments of contemplation, Storm said, "Get us closer, but don't make it obvious. We don't want to be seen." With that, the scarred-faced man turned from the windscreen and to the navigator's table. Pinned upon it were exterior schematics of the Goliath airship. As he studied the illustration Brock stepped up beside him and pointed at the plans.

"The way I see it, you've got a much better chance of connecting the grapple with the frame here and at the engines. Why pick the smallest target?" he asked, indicating a tiny spot at the top of the port-side gasbag.

"If they've posted guards on the outside of this thing, they're going to be right at those other spots for their comfort. I'm sure none of these guys want to stand in the open air up here, especially in this weather," said

Storm as he viewed the drawings, trying to visualize what would come ahead, what he had to do. "I've got a better chance to be sneaky where I'm headed. Come on; help me into the grappling rig."

The tri-motor had been a standard airline model originally, but had undergone extensive modifications. On the outside, a pair of extra fuel tanks had been added to the wings and the hull widened slightly; inside, the cockpit had been extended to carry eight while the rear had been cleared of all passenger accommodations and was now used for pure cargo space; additional space had been added to the airframe for cargo as well. Storm and Brock moved to the equipment they'd been preparing on the floor of the plane. A large metal pack with a heavy-duty harness lay there beside another harness, which held a compressed air-tank and several utility pouches. Storm strapped on the pouch-and-tank harness, and then struggled into the heavy boxlike backpack with Brock's help.

Attached to the backpack was a gun-like tube that Storm strapped to his right forearm. At the end of this contraption was what nearly resembled a common toilet plunger, the bell of which was made of an odd black rubber-like material. This was studded with metallic protrusions.

As Storm was climbing into the harness and contraptions, he went over what was known of the situation in his mind: a group of gunmen armed with submachine guns had seemed to spring from nowhere shortly after the Goliath's maiden voyage had gotten underway and corralled the crew and passengers. In the confusion the radio operator, a young man named J.G. Smythe, had managed to send out a distress call, outlining what had happened. The unfortunate youth must have been discovered, however; he had been thrown overboard and his broken body was found in a field beneath the airship's flight path. Details had been sketchy, but what was known from Smythe's distress call was that the hijackers were foreign and probably European, although their exact nationality had not been disclosed by the transmission, if it was known at all by the radio man. Storm wondered who they were. Were they German? Maybe. A lot of rumblings had come from Germany lately of a new political party that promised peace but carried an incredible threat to those who looked behind their proclamations. Were they some of Benito Mussolini's fascists, perhaps? Not likely. There weren't really any bad relations between the United States and Italy at the moment. Who could it have been, then? Regardless of who it was behind the attack, they obviously wanted the airship and its crew. They wanted the passengers as well. Aboard were some pretty powerful people from business and political circles, people worth lots of money for their influence and secrets. They wanted it badly enough to kill; Storm's mind flashed to the dead crew member and he grimaced. While the authorities waited on the ground and argued over what to do, more lives could be lost; action had to be taken now.

Storm strapped a holster to his thigh, the butt of a strange pistol protruding from it. Now he was ready.

Brock stepped back and stroked his handlebar mustache; he smiled bemusedly. "You look like a mountaineer from space."

"And I feel like a damned anvil," Storm grinned back. "I'm going to sink like a stone."

Storm donned a thick leather helmet and strapped a pair of goggles on his forehead. He moved forward again toward the cockpit. Ahead and below the Ford plane, the Goliath moved through the clouds. Peering through his binoculars, he could see no activity on the airship's frame and engine-pods, but he could picture snipers in his mind, crouching and watching the plane. They might not really be there, but yet they could be... His stomach was in knots but this had to be tried, had to be done...crazy or not.

"Okay, Skids. You know the drill."

With that, the diminutive pilot eased the throttle forward, bringing the plane even with the center of the airship, and then kept up with it while slowly lowering the plane's altitude. The two men listened through the storm and sounds of the engine, waiting for the sound of bullets clattering through the metallic skin of their Ford plane. The sounds had not come... yet.

After checking the situation one final time through the windscreen, Storm returned to the rear of the plane. Brock was already standing by the door and belted into the safety-harness there. The look on his face reminded Storm of an eager-to-please hound, patiently asking his master's permission to go with him.

"I wish I could help, Boss...I wish you'd let me help," he said. "I don't like you doing this alone."

"I wish you could help me too, Brock," he replied. "But we only have one of these things, though. If anyone is going to die doing this, I'd rather it be me." He clapped the huge muscle-man on the shoulder. "Now open the damn door for me."

Brock smiled. "Good luck, Boss," he said, then wrenched open the door.

It suddenly seemed as though the wind and rain and lightning were trying to reach inside the plane as a howling filled the Ford and Skids fought to keep it steady. Storm gripped the safety handles in the frame with white knuckles, staring down at the top of the Goliath below, at the tiny spot he would aim for.

"Break a leg!" Skids called from the pilot's cabin, his voice small and barely heard above the shrieking wind.

"If only it was just my leg that could get broken," Storm thought as he battled to get his stomach under control. He pulled the goggles down over his eyes. "What if a freak gust of wind hits me?" he thought. "What if I misjudge the calculations? What if the grappler fails? What if there are snipers?

"What if, what if, what if...?"

Clifton Storm silently said a prayer and jumped from the plane, feeling as if the hand of fate had finally caught him.

The raging weather whipped at Storm, his face stinging and red from the icy rain. He kept his arms tightly at his side, his legs together as he plummeted headfirst toward the blimp below. Ice rolled in the pit of his stomach, and despite the chill from the rain he now was drenched in cold sweat. He watched his target, the circular access bulkhead set into the airship's hull, growing in his vision. He seemed to be waiting an eternity until the moment he would be in range. He was nearly there...

Then disaster struck. A freak gust of wind hit him and he was blown off course, his arrow-like plunge pushed away from the dirigible, his trajectory now headed directly towards the soaking field far below.

Panic, like a caged beast, surged inside his body. Storm fought it under control, willing his mind back into the zone of cold command. He struggled to aim the contraption on his arm at the receding hatch. There was no time for calculations now, only for instinct and luck. He sighted along the tube and pressed the launch toggle.

Compressed air in the backpack was released with a deafening shriek as the tube on Storm's arm launched the plunger-like device at the hatch. It flew straight, trailing an unwinding coil of metallic cable, the other end of which was spooled in the backpack. The projectile missed the hatch but connected with the side of the hatch housing, a combination of vacuum and magnetic devices activating on their own to hold it fast.

But would it hold? The entire grappler assembly was untested...there had been no time for tests, even though the device had been in development for months. It had originally been conceived as precisely what it was being used as: an emergency air-to-air boarding device for someone to transfer from one aircraft to another. However, the model he was wearing was only the prototype. The scientists and inventors in his employ had just enough time to complete it before the Goliath had been hijacked by foreign agents on its maiden voyage. The grappler device was planned to eventually be scaled down, made smaller. The smaller size would allow the person using it to also wear a parachute in case something went wrong... but this was the prototype: it was still unproven and it was far too bulky for Storm to wear a parachute in addition to the device. He continued his sickening plunge toward the ground.

Suddenly, his fall past the airship stopped abruptly as the cable reached its end and became taut; the grappler held fast. His fall now became an arc. He smacked hard into the side of the Goliath, into the fabric-covered metal superstructure inside. He felt a queasy pop in the side of his body as the breath was knocked out of him. He groaned in pain.

"There goes a rib or two," he thought.

He dangled there for a moment, batted about by the wind and rain. He was in pain and shaky from the adrenaline rush, but he was still alive after the crazy attempt. He took a moment to rest and to collect himself before moving on.

Inside the Ford tri-motor, Brock sank back into the co-pilot's seat, its springs complaining. The pair of binoculars fell from his hand as he let out the breath he'd been holding.

"If we live through this, we are gonna get so drunk..." said Skids, his forehead beaded with perspiration.

"We still have a ways to go," said Brock, as he wiped his own brow. "This has only just started, and Cliff has to get in next."

He had watched Storm long enough to make sure the grapple-device worked and to make sure he was still alive. Now, he steeled himself and raised the binoculars to his eyes again...

After he got his second wind, Storm managed to turn toward the side of the blimp. He planted his feet and hit another toggle on the arm-device. The winch in the backpack began to turn winding the cable up with a grinding noise. He let it pull him up, climbing the side of the Goliath with agonizing slowness. He felt exposed and naked dangling out there in the wind and he kept darting glances to the possible enemy hiding spots; there could be snipers everywhere around him, watching him.

Reaching the top of the gigantic flying machine, Storm knelt by the access hatch and unstrapped the grappler pack. He removed the pistol from its holster, and then connected a hose from the air tank on his harness to the strange gun. With a twist of a valve and a low hiss, the air gun was ready for business, a magazine of deadly steel darts nestled in its grip. The motive behind the gun was simple: although the hijackers had surely not taken the same precautions, it was a good idea not to use flammable gun-powder weapons in a combustible atmosphere... such as a hydrogen-filled blimp. The flaming crash would be a tragedy, and Storm wanted to prevent it from becoming a reality as much as possible.

Storm turned the handle on the hatch, brief doubt flashing in his mind. What if it was locked? If it was locked, he would have to find a way to get around it. However, it turned completely and quietly, and he cautiously eased the hatch open and thrust the pistol's barrel down into the space beneath. Confident that no one was lurking and waiting just inside, he lifted the hatch all the way back on its hinges.

A narrow shaft was revealed, a ladder to one side descended into the darkness below.

There would be a long journey down, he thought. Down past the service walkways, past the gas-bags, all the way down to the bottom eighth of the Goliath, where over a hundred passengers and 20 crewmen were being held hostage by armed foreign spies.

It was unclear how many hijackers there were, their locations, armaments. It wasn't even clear if the passengers and crew were still alive. It was clear to Storm, however, that a massacre should be averted if it had not already occurred, and the Goliath be brought home.

Marshalling his resolve, he started down the ladder, closing the hatch above his head after stealing one last glance at the crimson and aluminum tri-motor following at a distance...

(from an Associated Press newspaper report)

"CHALLENGER" STORM DOES IT AGAIN

Tuesday September 19, 1933- Passengers and crew aboard the new and mighty airship *Goliath* found themselves in the middle of what most people experience only on the moving-picture screen or in their worst nightmares. At 10:00 am, the 114 passengers and 20 crew members boarded the *Goliath*, the biggest dirigible to date at over 800 feet long. The *Goliath* set sail from New Orleans, Louisiana, on its maiden voyage bound for its first stop in Atlanta, Georgia. Not one person on board knew what was in store for as they boarded the massive luxury craft.

At approximately 11:05 am a distress call from aboard *Goliath* alerted Mobile, Alabama officials to crisis aboard the giant dirigible. According to officials, 15 individuals of unknown origin had boarded the vessel and hidden themselves away in the cargo hold, unbeknownst to the staff and crew. The plotters forced all passengers and crew members into the dining room where they were kept hostage. After discovering the distress call had been made, the nefarious hijackers callously threw the radio operator, J.G. Smythe, from the craft and to his death. A cadre of Army Air Corps planes was dispatched to the horror in the sky, but due to a massive storm the visibility was next to impossible. The plotters, it seemed, were hiding in the tempest.

The mysterious and well-known freelance troubleshooter Clifton Storm then perpetrated a daring mid-air boarding maneuver. After eliminating 6 of the hijackers in his brave rescue efforts, Storm then rallied the passengers and crew to assist in detaining the other 9 plotters. This occasion is the third high-profile rescue by the mystery-man Storm, whom the media has already dubbed "Challenger."

The *Goliath* landed safely at the Montgomery, Alabama, airport at approximately 1:00 pm. Apart from the unfortunate radio man, no injuries were reported for the passengers and crew; however, according to the shipboard doctor, Storm suffered a knife wound to the shoulder and two broken ribs in his brave efforts to once again defend the innocent. Upon landing, Storm declined comment to newsmen and hurriedly boarded a small passenger plane, no doubt bound for his Miami, Florida, base of operations.

Government officials are holding the surviving hijackers in an undisclosed area for questioning. Meanwhile, State Department officials are in contact with Storm as the case develops.

The *Goliath* plans to set voyage again soon, and thanks once again to the valiant efforts of the mysterious "Challenger" Storm, she'll be back in the sky in no time.

CHAPTER 1:
THE HUNTED MAN

Gordon Tolliver parted the curtains of his dark hotel room and looked out onto the street below. Five stories down, a dark sedan sat by the curb like any other car. The sedan was occupied, however. Tolliver had watched the glowing tips of cigarettes inside the car ever since darkness fell at the beginning of the evening. He knew the car's occupants were waiting for him.

Tolliver knew that getting help would mean disaster and death for both his daughter Kate and himself. However, it was a risk he had to take and he was running out of time to do it. He considered stopping his quest for assistance, considered turning tail and going back and letting himself get taken back by the men who had followed him home to the U.S. from that accursed land. He knew he had come too far, though. He had passed the point of no return and too much was riding on him now.

He dressed in the darkest suit he owned and pulled his hat down low. For extra resolve he took a shot of the bathtub gin he had snuck in with his luggage, feeling the withering liquid fire course down his throat and into his belly. His body relaxed a bit, and he looked at himself in the mirror. The image looking back at him was of an iron-grey-haired man, lines of age creasing a firm visage. His body was still fit and healthy for a man his age, his countenance was the confident and intelligent face that had faced countless opponents on the battlefields of the boardroom. But his eyes… his eyes showed the weariness he felt; the miles and the stress were beginning to dig in and take hold on him. He knew he couldn't keep up the mental strain much longer. "Forget the exhaustion," he thought to himself. "You can do this." He took a deep breath and left his hotel room.

The hallways were cool and quiet and he expected each doorway to hold an assailant, a pistol-clutching fist and a deadly pair of eyes. There was no one to confront him in the hallway, however, and apart from a smiling, vacationing young couple that passed him it seemed deserted. He eschewed the elevator and descended the back staircase; he knew someone was perhaps already in the hotel looking for him and he did not want to show himself. He set his jaw and looked for an alternative way out of the hotel; he knew where he had to go but getting there could be a problem and he had to pick his path carefully. Each step could be a pitfall, each corner could be into a blind alley of failure and capture.

He found the service entrance at the back of the hotel and paid the staff he found there to let him out and to forget his face. He hoped his pursuers, if there were any, wouldn't pay more than the fifty dollars he'd given to the freckled young man with the eager eyes.

The near-silence of the hotel gave way to a mélange of sensations as he stepped into the alleyway. The Florida night was cool, a contrast to the warm October day that had come before. The smell of slow-cooking pork and mojo spices wafted to his nostrils, and the sound of the distant and crowded street was mixing with a band playing a rumba somewhere. He was smack in the middle of the busiest hotel section of the tourist-choked Miami autumn.

Cautiously, he made his way to the end of the alley and stepped onto the sidewalk. He meshed himself in with the passing crowds as well as he could, but the lurking fear and danger still hung on him. His eyes darted towards the people, the passing cars, doorways, windows. He was wary of every person, every sound. His face showed fatigue, but inside he drew strength from the thought of his daughter and the others that depended on him.

Tolliver hailed a passing cab, hoping the car that sat in front of the hotel was the only one that was prowling and hunting for him. He got in and named his destination address to the cabbie, and as the cab pulled into traffic he twisted to look through the rear window, searching the street behind the taxi for possible trailing people or vehicles.

After a few minutes of craning his head in alert watchfulness, the tired man rubbed his eyes. Fatigue was creeping up on him again, stronger this time, and he felt as though he was slowly easing into a warm bath. Sleep would be so welcome to him right now, so peaceful and blissful and all-encompassing. Closing his eyes, he rested his head on the back of his seat. The sound of the car's engine lulled him gently, and the world seemed to drop away as the darkness behind his eyes grew deeper and deeper...

"Hey!"

The startled cabbie's shout snapped Tolliver to attention and he sat bolt-upright. His eyes opened and shot to the side window just in time to see another car, this time a dark-colored coupe, as it crossed over and into the cab's lane on a collision course. The driver of the taxi expertly swerved his car around the menacing coupe and swore.

"What the hell?!"

The frightened passenger's head snapped around as they passed the coupe. Through the rear window he could see the ugly sneers of the two men in the coupe's front seat... and the muted glint of a Tommy gun in the backseat.

Frightened, he sunk down low in the taxi's backseat. "Try to lose them! Get me to a crowded corner, please!" he pleaded.

The driver accelerated his cab and cocked a crooked grin. "Wonder what the devil you did, pal. These guys sure as hell want you."

"Please, just drive!" the hunted man urged him, craning his neck to peer over the back seat and into the street behind them.

Weaving in and out of traffic, they soon left the pursuing car behind. The cab rounded a corner ahead, tires screeching against the pavement and they came to an open-air nightclub. Dancers whirled in pairs to a lively charanga orchestra under colored lights strung from the surrounding roofs. The people here were dense, tightly packed and in constant motion... a great place to get lost in.

"Crowded enough for ya'?" the cabbie shouted back.

"Yes, stop here." Tolliver dropped a fistful of bills into the front seat. The cabbie saw it from the corner of his widened eyes, but he kept them on the road. It looked to be triple the amount of the fare.

The cab slowed to a stop and Tolliver launched himself into the crowd, his head held low as he tried to lose himself in the festive atmosphere. Several seconds later, the coupe pulled up to the curb and the passengers hurriedly piled out. The driver continued down the road, eyes sharp and searching through the thickly-packed crowds for J. Gordon Tolliver.

The tough-looking passengers wove their way through the crowd at the open-air nightclub. One thug kept his hand on the revolver in his coat pocket, the other held his Tommy gun beneath the long coat he wore; the duo were prepared for action and didn't care if anyone got in the way of their quarry. Their rough-shaven faces were browned by exposure to the sun, their features Hispanic. They searched for their prey as they prowled through the din and cluster of the nightclub patrons who reveled and danced around them, unaware of how close to death they could become.

Past the nightclub crowd, Tolliver found a narrow passageway between two buildings that wound its way through an alley and to the street corner behind them. After checking the nearby traffic, he hurriedly grabbed another cab and gave his destination again. His heart was pounding and he was covered in sweat. The Miami night no longer felt cool; it now felt hot and humid, and it felt like walls were closing in all around him... it had become oppressive, and it reminded him of the tropical heat elsewhere, in the place where his troubles had all begun.

The cab drove on, and the minutes ticked by in dark silence. The vehicle soon left the main congestion of the city behind it as it headed south, the city slowly giving way to lush trees and a cooling breeze. To the left, the moonlight was sparkling on the dark waves of Biscayne Bay and could be seen intermittently through the palms. Eventually, the lights of the Pan American seaplane airport could be seen ahead and on the left; the cab passed this facility. Not long after they passed the airport, they came to their destination: a private airfield. The sign on the front gate read "Miami Aerodrome Research and Development Laboratories," beneath it a smaller sign read "C. Storm & Associates: Troubleshooters." The dark compound of buildings and airstrips was where his hope for assistance lay, and the scared and tired passenger could barely believe he had made it there alive and in one piece. Tolliver told the cabbie to stop just shy of the gate, and the cab braked to a halt. The passenger climbed from the car and paid his driver with a generous tip, then strode toward the guardhouse beside the gate as the vehicle drove on back to the city. Tolliver habitually smoothed his clothes out as he walked, while elation and nervous tension were mixing inside his stomach.

Benny the security guard looked up from the radio he was tuning inside the little building and he regarded the late-night visitor warily. Tolliver gave his name to him, and then said "I believe Clifton Storm is expecting me."

"Hang on," said Benny, as he lifted the receiver of his telephone. He plugged a cord into a small switchboard beside the desk. "I think he went out a while ago, and I haven't seen him in a while," Benny said as he listened to the ringing of the phone on the other end.

Disappointment clouded Tolliver's face. "I talked to him on the telephone earlier today. I hope he hasn't forgotten about meeting me tonight."

Tense seconds passed in silence. In the distance, from the lights of the city came the headlights of a car driving up the road, but nothing moved otherwise. The night seemed to wait expectantly.

"There's no answer," Benny said finally, setting the receiver back down. "You want to come in and wait here with me until he gets back?'

Disappointment and anxiety still clung to the hunted man. "Okay, yes," he nodded

Benny unlocked the gate, which was kept closed at night, and it squeaked open for Tolliver to enter.

Suddenly, the car that had been heading up the road turned sharply. The engine roared and it rocketed toward the gate.

It was the pursuing coupe!

Tolliver jumped through the gate just before the car struck it. Benny also leaped out of the way, drawing his revolver from his belt holster as he leapt. Shots from inside the car were launched at Benny but went wide and missed the wiry security man. Meanwhile, Tolliver began running for the dark buildings inside the compound. He was fit and active for his age but the coupe was gaining on him and he was slower from fatigue.

Taking careful aim, Benny shot out one of the car's tires and it fish-tailed and skidded to a stop abruptly. Benny had fired all the rounds in his revolver, and as he hurried to reload the man in the back of the coupe leaped out of the car. His Tommy gun began chattering flame toward the guardhouse. Hastily, Benny dove into the shelter of the doorway, but the hail of bullets kept him at bay. He was powerless to help the hunted man.

Meanwhile, the two men who had sat in the front of the car had sprung from their seats and had begun chasing Tolliver on foot. Suddenly, their quarry slipped and fell, and one of the pursuing men caught up to him. As Tolliver struggled to get up the attacker bludgeoned him in the back of the head with the butt of his pistol. Tolliver fell back down, stunned, and the world seemed to whirl around his head, fuzzy and indistinct.

Smugly, the two thugs stooped to pick the fallen man up. To Tolliver's aching and dizzy eyes, the men seemed to tower over him like giants. They grinned in triumph.

Headlights suddenly blazed over the scene as a sedan- the same dark-colored car that had sat in front of Tolliver's hotel- plowed past the ruined metal gate. A trio of figures leaped from the car, each one attacking one of the would-be pursuers.

To Tolliver's blurring vision, it seemed as though the new combatants

"Benny also leaped out of the way."

were super-human, and it was hard to take in what was happening. A huge hulking figure picked up the machine gunner and drove him through the rear window of the coupe as though he were a limp rag doll. Meanwhile a swift dark figure grabbed and slugged one of the men standing over Tolliver as he was trying to pull a gun. The thug wove on his feet momentarily then launched a haymaker punch at the other man, who swatted it aside and connected with his own; the thug spun and went down. The third new combatant tackled the thug who had pistol-whipped Tolliver. The two scuffled on the ground and the thug suddenly untangled himself and stood, drawing aim with his pistol his attacker. The man on the ground lashed out with his foot, striking the pistol and knocking it away, then swung his leg back the other way and connected with the thigh of the gunman. He collapsed and the savior struck a strange blow to the side of the thug's head with the palm of his hand. The thug groaned and stopped moving, unconscious.

All was suddenly quiet and still. The three saviors surrounded the pursued man as he lay on the ground. Benny ran up and joined them.

"He said his name is Tolliver," Benny said to the tackler. "He said you were expecting him." The man to whom Benny had been speaking knelt down, his scarred face lit by the headlights, and looked into Tolliver's eyes.

"We went to meet him, to grab him as soon as he came out of the hotel. We were worried that there were guards inside. Damn it, we should've watched the back, too."

As he was lifted up off of the ground by the men, understanding dawned on Tolliver. He tried to smile, but unconsciousness claimed him before his lips could twitch and he finally fell into that delirious black silence of sleep.

CHAPTER 2: INTRODUCTION

Colliver opened his eyes to painfully bright sunlight. It was streaming through a window and Venetian blinds to his left, and a slight creaking sound came from the spinning ceiling fan above him. He was groggy and his head was aching, and he had a hard time getting his bearings.

Where was he?

Slowly it came back to him. The previous night, the hotel room, the chase through Miami streets, his arrival at the Miami Aerodrome complex, the attack, and his rescue... it all seemed like some distant dream, some half remembered story he'd been told third-hand. He was now lying in a bed, clad in his shorts and undershirt. The white sheets were cool and crisp against his skin. At the foot of the bed, neatly laid out on a chair, was his suit; it had been cleaned of the mud and dirt he'd fallen in the night before and was spotless. Beside the bed and chair, there was a wardrobe, a writing table and a radio. Otherwise the room was sparsely decorated and gave no hint of his location. The door was closed and no sounds came from the other side of it.

He got up and the sudden throbbing in the back of his head forced him sit back down on the bed. His hand touched the back of his head tenderly and he looked around again. The clock on the writing table indicated 10:18 am. Bewildered, he got up again, slower this time; he dressed before creeping softly out of the unlocked room.

The hallway outside was sterile and white, and the only sound was a faint humming of machinery somewhere. There were a few other doors set in the hallway. These were closed, but to the left was a large open room, a lounge of sorts containing a bookshelf, two sofas, and a low table littered with magazines and newspapers.

Tolliver followed the hallway, passing several branching passages until the hall widened. Here there were several laboratory rooms fronted by wide glass windows. Three of these were occupied, and he looked in on the white-coated men within each one for a moment.

In the first room were two bespectacled men: a sandy-haired man with a pipe clenched between his teeth and the other grey-haired and older. The one with the pipe was holding up a human skull, while the older scientist was making notations on it in blue pencil.

In the next room, a young Hispanic scientist was carefully mixing chemicals. As he turned toward a rack of vials, his sleeve caught a beaker full of liquid, which tumbled and shattered on the floor. The room began to fill with a noxious-looking gas. Riveted, Tolliver watched as the scientist reappeared in the billowing fogginess wearing a gas-mask. He activated an exhaust fan set into the wall and began to sweep up the glass fragments of the smashed beaker. His loud cursing was audible to Tolliver, despite the gas-mask and thick window.

Across the hall was the third occupied lab, although Tolliver mistook it for empty at first as it was nearly dark inside. Lit only by a Bunsen burner, the tall scientist inside, who wore a welding helmet and thick gloves, was working with powders. He added them to an oddly-shaped beaker of liquid that he was warming on the burner. The scientist turned on the light switch and Tolliver could see that the beaker of liquid was really an ordinary cup of coffee. The scientist lifted the helmet's face plate and began to drink it; leaning back in his chair, he began to thumb through the latest issue of *The Shadow* magazine...

The door at the end of the hall opened, spilling sunshine into the building. Tolliver blinked into the light as it awakened a new wave of pain in his aching skull. Framed in the doorway was a short blonde man in a leather jacket, a folded newspaper under his arm.

"Hey, Rip Van Winkle. Glad to see you're awake."

He strode over to Tolliver and extended a handshake. "I'm Manny Gerard, but most people here just call me 'Skids.' I heard you took a nasty bop to the head last night. How are you feelin'?"

Reflexively, Tolliver touched the lump that had formed behind his ear. "I have a horrible headache today, but I'm alive. Thank you, Mr. ... er, Skids."

"That's the spirit, Mr. Tolliver." Skids grinned as he clapped the older man on the back. "Our staff medic, Doc Foster, said you'll be just fine.

We'll get you some coffee and donuts and aspirin at the main office, that'll perk you up." He turned, and Tolliver followed him, smiling slightly. Skids' joviality was infectious.

Skids led the way through the door and outside. Once over the threshold, he announced to Tolliver in his best tour-guide voice: "Welcome to the Miami Aerodrome Research and Development Laboratories... or MARDL for short, since it can be quite a mouthful to say it otherwise." He grinned. "You get the grand tour, Mr. T.

"Of course, we just left the labs," he continued, waving his hand back at the building. "The folks in there work closely with our boss and are always busy working on something neat. They're experts; every last one of them is a leader in their field. Some of the stuff they're messing with in there is just downright scary, and some of their other projects I can't even pronounce. We're just damned glad to have them on our side, and if their knowledge fell into the wrong hands, we'd all be in for it." Tolliver turned and looked at the building that they had just left, surprised at how large it actually was: five stories high and as long and wide as a football field. There were very few windows, and these were mostly located at the rear and the top two floors.

Behind this building was a large warehouse (Skids indicated this was the supplies and materials building), and beside that there was another large structure that was fronted with huge rolling doors. "That huge building over there's the workshop and manufacturing area, where they put together our planes and equipment and stuff," Skids said, indicating the gargantuan building with the large doors. "What I said about the scientists goes for the engineering guys too: they work with Storm on various projects, all for the goal of making things better for everyone."

They walked on. The compound was laid out in a rough semi-circle, and Skids was walking Tolliver out of his way on the "tour": this served not only to show off the MARDL base of operations, but also to clear Tolliver's head a bit more before his meeting with Clifton "Challenger" Storm. It was a clear autumn day, warm and idyllic, and there wasn't a cloud in the sky.

Skids led him toward the compound's three main hangars and pointed them out, and as they walked past these Tolliver looked inside and noted the large number of mechanics and technicians inside. Skids gestured at them with the newspaper he carried. "More of the lifeblood here," he said. "The magazines and papers and newsreels may talk a lot about one or two of us high-profile types here, but those guys in there...they're our nuts and bolts. They hold everything we do together."

"Speaking of newspapers..." Tolliver said gesturing towards the one the pilot was holding. "In that photograph there… Is that you?"

Skids looked to where the older man was pointing to on his newspaper. A large picture was facing out from the sports page: it showed Skids- his grinning face grimy with engine oil and his normally perfect hair in disarray- clutching a large cup-like trophy. A statuesque blonde was on each arm, and a racing plane was parked behind him. The blondes were several inches taller than he was.

"Heh... Yeah, that's me." Skids said with confidence and sheepishness mixing in his voice. "I just won the Regionals yesterday. To the winner goes the spoils, huh, Mr. T?" Skids was proud of his air-racing accomplishments, and relished yet another excuse to bring one of his wins up in conversation.

"Don't listen to him," a voice boomed, "Those blonde 'spoils' wouldn't have given him the time of day if it wasn't for the photo opportunity."

They turned at the sound of the deep voice. A muscular and bald man was striding past them and toward the supply warehouse, a bundle of steel pipes over his shoulder. Beneath his mustache was the grin of a child who was up to no good, and an ever-present twinkle was in his eye.

"That's Brock Thurman." Skids said with a mock look of disgust on his face. "If you ever forget his name, just look for it in his tattoos. He's got it there just in case he forgets how to spell it." He said this joking comment loud enough for Brock to hear it; the mountainous man just laughed and kept walking.

"Nah, Brock's a good guy," Skids continued to the older man as they resumed their walk. "We just give each other hell now and then. He was in the circus once, and he's as strong as a damned ox. That guy would risk his neck for me and for any of us, though, and I'd do the same too if it came down to it." Tolliver now recalled the dim memory of Brock smashing the machine gunner through the car window the night before. He had seemed to do it with no more effort than if he'd tossed a pillow through the air.

In the next hangar they came to, Skids pointed amidst the crowd of technicians and to a thin black man with salt and pepper hair who was somewhere in his late fifties or early sixties. He was working on a propeller assembly and giving orders to the men around him. "That's Willy Avis," he said. Tolliver remembered the head mechanic's swift form taking down one of his attackers on the previous night with his rapid trip-hammer blows. "If Cliff Storm is the heart of this operation, then Willy is the brain. He's a mechanic deluxe who could make a palm tree fly." Skids waved to Willy, who returned the salute.

Tolliver, along with the rest of the world, had heard of Challenger Storm's assistants: a group of men and women who helped him on his adventures. Some of these troubleshooters appeared alongside their boss with more frequency than others did, but usually it was never the same exact group of aides to appear twice. They were all said to be skilled in their fields, but more prone to action-oriented professions than the scientists and engineers who worked behind the scenes at the MARDL laboratories and workshops. Skids, Brock, and Willy were some of these people of action, and Tolliver reflected on some of the stories and tall tales he had heard about Storm's crew of danger-loving comrades and wondered how true they were…

Somewhat outside of the semi-circle and in the distance beyond the hangars, Tolliver noted a low dark warehouse, but Skids didn't point out this building. Tolliver said nothing of his curiosity for the ominous-looking building and its contents, but noted the only decoration on the mysterious building: it was the same symbol that was everywhere in the compound. Buildings, coveralls, equipment, airplanes… all were decorated with the ubiquitous symbol: a wrench turning a bolt, flanked by a pair of black and grey wings.

"Mr. Gerard… er, Skids… Storm runs quite a facility here," Tolliver said. "How does he do it? An independent series of laboratories and development facilities is one thing, but an independent trouble-shooting business… doesn't the government ever step in to regulate things?"

Skids simply grinned and said, "So far we seem to have somebody that's up in a high place and on our side, Mr. T. Nobody has given us an official blessing yet… but nobody has tried to stop us, either. Apparently what we do here is okay in their book… it's okay in a lot of people's book, it seems."

Tolliver somberly asked, "What about the three men that tried to stop me last night? What happened to them?"

"Those guys," Skids snorted, "They're being held by the Miami police department. The boss went down there this morning, and the cops have been givin' them the third degree, trying to make 'em talk… but they're tough nuts to crack. They haven't uttered a single word about anything. In the meantime, we're going to see about helping you out with whatever they were chasing you for." With that, they turned and moved on.

In the distance and facing the crescent shape of the complex, beyond a high chain-link fence topped with barbed-wire, a sandy white beach and the blue waters of Biscayne Bay sparkled. Where the compound met the shore was a series of docks where various boats were bobbing up and down on the waves. There was also a seaplane hangar and taxiing into this was a Douglas Dolphin, its nose decorated with the painting of a black-haired woman wearing a grass-skirt and a flower in her hair...and little else, although the pose was not explicit. Painted next to her was the plane's name: Island Girl. Tolliver had noticed that many of the noses of other MARDL aircraft he'd seen were also decorated in a similar fashion, and he asked Skids about it.

"Yeah, the boss is a little superstitious about his planes, so he names them and has a pretty girl painted on their noses. Sometimes a little Peruvian guy named Al does the paintings for him when he passes through Miami, although he's gotten a few others to do work on the planes as well."

Skids waved his hands vaguely towards the trio of runways that criss-crossed near the center of the compound. "Some towers, some runway, et cetera... all really exciting stuff," he said sarcastically. They turned back toward the last structure: a three-story building that was apparently a combination of administration housing and control and radio tower. Outside of it a man in rolled-up shirt-sleeves was throwing a ball for a black-and-white dog. The dog scampered after the ball, skidded to a stop as he caught it and ran back to his master eagerly, eyes bulging and stubby tail wagging excitedly.

"And this," Skids explained, "is Clifton Storm...and Buddy. Hey Bud!" he called to the dog and whistled.

When the dog heard Skids call him, he came running and jumped into the aviator's arms. Meanwhile Storm smiled warmly and walked over to shake hands with Tolliver, who recognized the handsome but scarred countenance from the previous night and from the few news photographs that had managed to capture it. The pictures, however, didn't do justice to his actual presence, which was an almost tangible force.

"I'm very pleased to finally meet you, Mr. Tolliver... formally, that is," Storm said. "You gave everybody the slip last night, including us. Quite a scare too; you're lucky we decided to head back here when we did."

"I'm sorry about that, Mr. Storm," Tolliver said sheepishly. "I had been awake for nearly three days straight. I was tired of hiding, tired of waiting..."

"It's alright, Mr. Tolliver," Storm interrupted gently. "We've got you here now, and that's all that matters. Let's go to my office and get some coffee into you. I'm eager to hear your story."

CHAPTER 3:
A TALE OF RANSOM

Bidding a goodbye to Skids (who was now occupied with playing fetch with Buddy), Tolliver followed Clifton Storm into the main office. The cool reception room was spotlessly clean and formal, personalized only by a vase of purple flowers on the window sill and the clown doll on the desk. Behind this desk was an attractive and plump secretary with sparkling blue eyes and a ready smile. She was dressed quite fashionably, and Clifton Storm introduced her as Marie. "I would be lost without her," he said, smiling. "She manages paperwork- about a ton and a half of it- and that keeps us in the air." The red-headed secretary smiled and winked at Tolliver through her glasses, then continued typing.

Tolliver followed Storm into the next room, which was a complete opposite of the neat and tidy chamber they had just left. A large mahogany desk was piled with papers, books, charts, diagrams, photographs, newspapers, file folders, and other various pieces of debris, and beside the desk stood a large antique globe. Three walls of the room were covered in bookcases of varying size and mismatched design, and these held volumes of an astounding array of topics, seemingly arranged in no particular order or classification. The wall behind the desk was covered in maps and charts, and these were scrawled and dotted with notes and figures.

Storm motioned to the single chair opposite the desk, and as Tolliver sat down he realized that Storm's dog, Buddy, must have broken away from Skids' game of fetch and had been following them into the administration building. After he entered the room, he promptly trotted over and curled up on the palette of folded blankets next to Storm's desk. From around the corner he looked up at Tolliver with his large, sad eyes.

Storm left for a moment and then returned with a steaming cup of coffee for each of them. He closed the door, then sat and scratched Buddy's head, and the Boston terrier sighed and put his head down.

Storm swiveled his chair toward Tolliver and leaned back, his fingers forming a steeple in front of him as he rested his elbows on his desk. "Mr. Tolliver..." he began. "What can we do for you?"

Tolliver took a deep breath. He considered again for a moment that he could stop this now. He could get up and leave and not bring outside help into the snare he found himself in. He could refuse this chance at help and continue on as he had.

He refused this consideration and steeled his resolve.

"Mr. Storm," he began, "I wanted to meet you because I need your help. Do you know who I am?"

"Of course. You're James Gordon Tolliver, 63 years old. You're the head of White Heron Aviation and a pioneer in the construction of all-metal aircraft chassis. Recently you headed up the construction of the government's Valkyrie bomber project. Although the design never got past the prototype phase, it was hailed as a masterpiece of aeronautical engineering by those in the know. You're a widower of twelve years now, with one grown child: Katherine Alice, aged 23, schoolteacher."

Tolliver's eyes were wide; his jaw hung open slightly and he closed it and smiled. "Well, you've certainly done your homework."

Storm reassured him with a smile. "Standard procedures," he explained. "When we get a call for help from someone who claims to be in danger, we want to make sure we know who we'll be dealing with."

Storm's eyes probed the older man's. He could see the turmoil and fear that had forced him to ask for aid... along with something else, something that he couldn't identify. "Go on, Mr. Tolliver," he said, setting the intuitive feeling aside for now.

As Tolliver shifted nervously in his chair before resuming, Storm took his impressions of the older man in: he was tall, retaining the physique that his college rowing team had built when he was younger. He had heard plenty of tales of Tolliver's business savvy, and his personality wasn't necessarily forceful, but he did have a very confident reputation. He didn't seem to be the kind of man who would run often from his problems. "Asking for help doesn't come easily to a man like this," thought Storm. But the wide forehead and the firm set of his jaw showed the creative, strategic, and analytical brain inside. He had probably considered his options very carefully before making up his mind.

Again, Tolliver drew a deep breath. "It's actually my Katherine that I come to you for help with. She is a schoolteacher, as you said, but recently she's been teaching in smaller, 'third-world' countries. Her most recent assignment placed her in a tiny village on the island of La Isla de Sangre."

Inwardly, Clifton Storm grimaced at this bit of information. The little South American nation of La Isla de Sangre was well known and in the news recently... for unfortunate reasons. The ruling government there was poor, and although the royal family of the island was respectable, many of the smaller town leaders and officials were thought to be corrupt. The tiny towns and villages were under constant attack, caughtbetween the schemes and cross-fires of warring rebel factions. The country had been asking for aid from the League of Nations for several years, but the hostile nature of La Isla de Sangre had kept that aid from ever getting there. The island was in bad shape, a global hot-spot of conflict and despair.

Even the island's name was unfortunate: "La Isla de Sangre" meant "The Isle of Blood" in English. The island's name had been derived from the unusually vibrant red clay that was found everywhere there. From the hillsides to the jungle, whether in small patches or barren open stretches, the bloodily hued clay was all over the place. From the torrid state of the island's constant skirmishes, however, the name had come to take a more sinister meaning. It had been in constant states of violence for as long as anyone knew, and the Isle of Blood seemed cursed at its core.

"Katherine," Tolliver said, "is a smart and tough girl... she's stubborn, and she gets those qualities from me, I'm afraid," he smiled. "But she also has a gigantic heart and the strong desire to help people... and she got those from her mother." He looked out the window, eyes unfocused. Beyond the compound's fence there were swaying palms on the white beach, gulls circling above. Through the door, he could hear the clacking of Marie's typwrier as she worked, and Buddy snored softly from beside the desk. Everything here seemed quiet and peaceful... so far removed from that island hell where Katherine was.

Tolliver focused, coming out of his reverie. "Katherine's teaching means the world to her, and it means even more to all the people that she's helped there. Richard and I are so proud of her."

"Richard?" Storm asked. This was a name that hadn't been found in the research that he and his team had turned up.

"Oh, that's Richard Stein, Katherine's fiancé. He works for White Heron as a test pilot, and he relocated to the island to be with her. He sometimes comes to the States for assignments and special projects while she stays there working. She's educating both the children and the adults there, and her efforts will no doubt advance the prosperity of La Isla de Sangre's future."

"It's been said that knowledge is power." Storm took a sip of coffee.

"Yes it has, and that saying really is true... and that's the problem."

Tolliver looked down into his coffee before continuing. "The Villalobos Brothers are vicious warlords. There are two of them—Jorge and Esteban— and they and their forces control a private army that holds the northwestern portion of the island at its mercy. It's the most populated area of La Isla de Sangre, the poorest... and it's also where Katherine is. The Villalobos Brothers know that one of their footholds comes from the lack of education that much of the populace has. It's the key to keeping the citizens subdued and afraid to rise up and defend themselves.

"And because of her efforts to help and aid those who wouldn't have a chance, the Villalobos Brothers have developed a dislike for my Katherine."

Tolliver looked out the window again, this time his eyes were hard and flinty. Storm watched him closely. Tolliver cursed himself out loud for waiting so long before contacting help.

"Those bastards... they threatened her first, and she resisted. They burned down the schoolhouse, and she had the classes moved to another building. They shot at the window of her hotel room... so she got a hold of a shotgun to protect herself with." He smiled for a moment proudly. "My daughter does not give up very easily."

The tight-lipped smile he wore faded now. "They got her, though... Villalobos gunmen stormed into the new schoolhouse and attacked her, kidnapped her right in front of her afternoon class. One of the children tried to stop them... he was shot dead by one of the kidnappers. He was only 11 years old."

There was a silence that hung in the air now. It seemed to press upon them, like a physical force, like a thick liquid that filled their ears. Tolliver gulped his coffee, and then met again the steady gaze of Clifton Storm.

"They're holding her for ransom, Mr. Storm," he continued soberly. "My daughter means the world to me, but these thugs, these animals... they are asking for regular payments of $10,000 a month... a substantial amount, even for someone of wealth like you or I. These are payments to keep her alive..." He trailed off.

Outwardly, Storm showed no emotion. Inwardly, however, he felt the urge... a constant yearning he held to help the helpless and to punish those who prey upon them. It was a promise he'd made to himself and to the world a long time ago... a promise he swore to keep until he drew his last breath.

"Mr. Storm... help me." Tolliver pleaded. "Help me get my Katherine back. I can pay you whatever you require..."

"My people and I don't work for money, Mr. Tolliver," Storm assured him, his voice confident. "Nor do we work for any glory or fame. We do the things we do so that people like you and your daughter can live without terror. We will help you, but we'll require your presence and assistance on La Isla de Sangre. Are you up to it?"

"O-of course I'll help you," the tycoon hastily agreed. "Whatever you need of me, you have it at your disposal."

Clifton Storm smiled and stood, and Buddy snuffled awake and stretched beside him. The adventurer extended his hand to Tolliver, who took it in a firm handshake. "I'll have someone escort you to the hotel to get your things. We'll get set to leave as soon as you return."

Tolliver thanked him again, and then left for the front gate while Storm paged Skids to meet him there over the complex's intercom and loudspeaker system. He then sat back down and looked down at Buddy, who looked back up with eager eyes and a wagging tail.

There was something else, a feeling that there was more to the story. It tugged at Storm's mind as he began mental preparations for the journey to La Isla de Sangre.

He was still mulling over this intuition when the phone on his desk rang, jarring him from his reverie. Someone had dialed his personal extension.

CHAPTER 4: AN UNWELCOMING COMMITTEE

After the bright and crisp morning, the day seemed as though it was going to remain pleasant. As Skids drove Tolliver out of the MARDL compound and into the city the day brightened even further, and Tolliver's mood was elevated in spite of his gloom. He told Skids his story as he had related it to Storm earlier and the two men discussed the situation, eventually turning to pleasant small-talk as they drove on. The idyllic Miami mood eased the tycoon's mind, and he didn't mind the light discussions about current events. Such pleasantries almost gave Tolliver a sense of normalcy, even though he knew it was temporary. In the back of his mind all that had happened remained, and there was no running from it no matter how sunny and nice the atmosphere and the company was being.

The grey coupe pulled up in front of the hotel, and Skids waved to a pair of lounging cops out in front of the art deco building. They waved back. Storm and his men were becoming quite well known and respected by the citizens of Miami, and the MARDL troubleshooters were on a first-name basis with many members of the Miami police department. The flyer and Tolliver climbed the steps and entered the hotel's spacious lobby through the large glass doors. As they passed by the patrons lounging in the lobby's comfortable chairs, they failed to notice the pair of eyes that was watching them intently over a newspaper from the corner…

Skids and Tolliver rode the elevator up to the fifth floor, stepping out into the lushly-carpeted hallway. It was as cool and as empty as it had been the night before when Tolliver had begun his flight from his room, but the businessman's fear had evaporated. He felt confident and safe now that he had Storm and his troubleshooters on his side. He turned his key in the lock of his room… and found that it was already unlocked, and the door swung easily inward.

Three men were waiting just inside the room. The furthest one away from the door stood over a bound and gagged figure in a chair: one of the hotel's maids. The young girl's eyes were wide with fear, her cheeks dark with tear-smeared mascara. The man held a revolver pointed at the girl's head and he smiled an ugly sneer at the two men, who found themselves covered now as well by the guns of the two other thugs just inside the door.

Tolliver was startled as he recognized the three men as his pursuers from the previous night's harrowing chase; they showed the bruises and wounds from their encounter with Storm and his men, but glared at him with triumph. His mind whirled with questions and the cold fire of fear burned in his stomach. Skids' hand shot to his own revolver in the holster beneath his leather jacket, but the feeling of another pistol's barrel pressing into his back stopped him cold. As the two men had left the elevator, they had failed to notice another man stalk noiselessly from the stairwell at the end of the hall behind them.

"Not so fast, blondie," the thug behind Skids growled in thickly accented English. "Get inside and get your hands up."

Skids and Tolliver did as they were commanded and stepped into the room. The fourth gunman stepped inside behind them and closed the door.

"We've come a long way to bring you back, *señor*," the thug beside the maid said. "We're not going home empty handed."

"You were stupid to get help," another one spoke up. He had bandages around his head from being hurled through the glass rear car window by Brock the night before, and looked like his mood was all the worse for the experience. "That's going to cost these two people their lives." He nodded toward Skids while waving his hand toward the trembling maid.

Skids started to respond with one of his quips but then he stopped himself. At this moment, the gunmen had the upper hand. From what the bandaged thug had said, he knew that the men planned on killing both him and the maid before taking off with J. Gordon Tolliver. The guns didn't have silencers, so the men were probably not going to do it in the hotel: the gunshots would bring unwanted attention. No, these men would probably

"..the man held a revolver to the girl's head.."

lead the three of them out as inconspicuously as possible to their vehicle. They would be taken someplace else- perhaps to a more deserted part of town, perhaps to one of the area's more isolated mangroves- and shot dead. Skids decided to play along for the time being and watch and wait for his chance to act. He wondered if the patrol men were still downstairs

"Okay, here's the plan," the gunman who had snuck up behind them said. "The seven of us are going for a little drive. You're going to play along, nice and smooth like, and walk with us. Don't try anything funny, because we'll be walking behind you with our pistols under our coats like this," the thug demonstrated. Skids suppressed a sardonic grin: they were doing exactly what he knew they would do. The other men, one by one, removed their own coats and draped them over their weapons while the man behind Skids reached into the pilot's jacket and removed his pistol: a Colt Peacemaker revolver.

"Look at this, eh?" the man, who seemed to be their leader, said to his companions. "This rod's bigger than he is."

The other three laughed, and Skids bristled inwardly. "Just wait... you're gonna get yours," he thought.

The procession moved out of the room and out into the hallway. Tolliver was in front, flanked by a pair of thugs. Behind them walked Skids on the right and the now unbound maid on the left. She had been made to wash her face of the smeared makeup and was now free from the tear-streaks, but was still as terrified as ever. Behind each one of these captives walked a thug— the one with the bandaged head behind the girl, the leader behind Skids. They were being walked to the stairwell at the end of the hall: the gunmen didn't want to chance an elevator operator spotting their pistols. They knew the group would look suspicious if examined too closely, and the captors didn't want the unwanted attention.

Even though the guns weren't pressed against them, the captives could each feel their presence at their backs as they walked: black holes of death staring at the targets like the dark eyes of the Devil. Skids thought frantically: he had to watch for any occasion, any moment when opportunity would present itself to allow him to fight back. He knew they wouldn't kill Tolliver: their aim was to take the aviation mogul back to La Isla de Sangre. The girl, however, was worthless to the gang and Skids knew the killers wouldn't care if she got caught in any fights that might erupt. The small pilot knew he had to stop their murderous plans, but first he knew he had to get her out of the way of danger first. Skids was on the alert, watching and waiting for just the right moment to make his move…

And then it happened: as they passed by an elevator, the cage clattered open to let a pair of hotel patrons out. In a blur of motion, Skids drew his foot up and stomped down hard upon the toes of the killer at his back, who shouted in pain as one of his toes snapped from the blow; Skids followed the foot-stomp with an elbow to the thug's nose. As he followed through he managed to pull his revolver from where it was tucked into the waist of the man's trousers with his other hand and fired a hasty shot at the maid's captor. The shot went wide but made the bandaged thug leap back for cover at the corner of an adjoining hallway. Skids hastily grabbed the maid and flung her across the hall and into the open elevator beside the shocked operator and the pair of hotel guests.

"Lobby!" he shouted to the operator. "Get the cops!" The wide-eyed operator nodded and did as he was told. He threw the doors shut and sent the cage and its four occupants rocketing back to the ground floor.

The previously empty hallway had suddenly filled with pandemonium. Patrons who had rushed into the passage when they heard the shots now panicked and fled for their rooms or down the stairwell at the end of the hall. The other gunmen had sprung into action. One of Tolliver's captors now held the tycoon in front of him with a choking arm around his neck, his pistol pressed against the side of Tolliver's head. The other thug with Tolliver had turned and was covering the hallway with his pistol. The gunman with the sore foot had recovered from his stumble, his face covered in blood, and he raised his pistol at Skids, who dove toward the closed door at opposite the elevator. The bullet struck the wall as his shoulder hit the door: it splintered at the lock and flew inward. The room behind the door was dark and unoccupied, and the little pilot twisted nimbly as he fell into the room. He landed on his back, Colt raised and ready as the bloody-faced killer filled the doorway for just a moment. It was all the time needed. Skids fired, a hot slug crashing through the thug's forehead. He straightened, wide-eyed, and collapsed before the ragged hole between his eyes began to bleed.

Meanwhile, the third killer had emerged from his cover in the side-hall and was coming toward the room that held Skids. He called out to his companions in Spanish, and Skids knew that the other two were going to try and rush from the hotel with Tolliver as their hostage. He had to try and stop them.

Skids sprang to his feet and ran for the doorway, only to be forced to jump back into the hotel room as the killer in the hall fired a shot at him. He felt helpless and trapped, and he hoped the pair of cops they had passed in the street outside the hotel were still there and were responding to the shots…

The cops, as it happened, had just finished their lunch and had been climbing into their radio squad-car when they were stopped by the sound of screams. Looking up, they witnessed the swarm of hotel patrons running out of the hotel lobby like rats from a sinking ship. "There's been shots fired inside!" one of the guests yelled to the blue-uniformed patrolmen. A young uniformed lift operator corroborated: "Up on the fifth floor!" he added.

The first cop, Officer Dan Kenton, leaned back into the car and began to radio the situation to headquarters but he was halted: coming from the radio was the dispatcher's voice… with orders for all cars in the area to converge on the very same hotel for a possible kidnapping in progress!

"Damn, that was fast!" Kenton said to his partner, Officer Terry Bergman, who nodded with bulging eyes. Kenton hurriedly radioed back to the station that they were on the scene then turned from the car. They drew their weapons and sprinted across the street and up the steps into the lobby, which was rapidly emptying of the remaining fleeing guests.

"That was one of Challenger Storm's men we saw going inside earlier," said Bergman as they ran. "Wonder if this has anything to do with him."

As soon as they were in the door, they ran past the empty front desk and for the elevators past it at the back. Suddenly, a form appeared there at the stairs around the corner, shabby-suited and dragging a grey-haired man by the throat. He had a pistol, and his eyes widened with surprise at the sight of the men in blue.

"Freeze!"

Kenton's shout as he leveled his service revolver at the captor echoed in the now empty lobby, but it only spurred the thug into his own action. He leveled his own weapon and fired, causing Kenton's own shot to go wide as the cops dove for cover. The gunman and his hostage whipped back behind the corner and leaned out again, taking advantage of his moment with the upper hand. He fired.

Bergman yelped in pain as the bullet tore through his right shoulder, and he dropped his weapon. Kenton overturned a nearby coffee table and the two policemen found themselves behind a temporary and flimsy wooden barricade. Taking a second to assess his partner's wound, Kenton found Bergman's shoulder rapidly spilling blood. The long-faced patrolman gritted his teeth in pain, and Kenton's pale blue eyes grew hard.

Kenton raised himself up on his elbow to get another shot at the kidnapper, but shrank back behind the table again as another bullet whistled past his ear. In that brief moment, he also caught a glimpse of a second gunman aiming at the pair, and knew his situation was becoming hopeless. Regardless, he managed to squeeze off another shot at the corner, and the pair of killers and their captive shrank back behind their cover for a moment. *Where the hell are those reinforcements?* Kenton wondered.

CHAPTER 5:
HELL HOTEL

There was a sudden roaring noise outside the lobby's doors, and it grew to a crescendo before something crashed through the glass portal. It was a motorcycle, and as it landed in the lobby the figure astride the machine leaped nimbly to the floor and into rapid action. Clifton Storm tossed a fat 2 ½ inch canister toward the back of the lobby at the startled kidnappers, and then dove behind the table with the cops to get clear of the aim of their weapons.

Back by the stairs, the canister burst with a "whoompf" sound, and the lobby was almost instantly filled with a strange cloud. It was luminous green, this cloud, but had the odd secondary effect of absorbing the ambient light from the room around it. The effect was of a ghostly fog that was somehow wrapped in an aura of darkness that even sunlight struggled to penetrate. The lobby now became surreal as the cloud billowed in all directions and the blinded thugs began cursing.

Storm yanked a pair of goggles from his forehead and down over his eyes, and the chemically-treated lenses instantly counteracted the effects of the bizarre smoke-grenade. Through the goggles, he had a nearly 100 percent clear view of his surroundings.

"Good work holding them off, Officer. Those men are blinded for now; can you find your way back to the door?"

"Yes," Kenton nodded. Through the green fog he could just barely make out Storm's familiar scarred face as he spoke to him.

"Good, you should gradually be able to see the doorway better as you near it. Now get your partner out of here," Storm instructed. "I'll give you some cover fire." With that, Storm crawled to where his motorcycle lay not far from the overturned table. From a leather holster on the side of the bike, he drew a Tommy gun and slapped a fresh drum of ammunition into place. Kenton stood, and supported the wounded Bergman with an arm around his shoulders.

"Go!" Storm commanded, and began to fire bursts from his submachine gun back toward the spot where he could see the thugs trying to peer around the corner and through the cloud. They ducked back behind cover as the two cops managed to hobble through the green fog and toward the door.

Storm kept up the intermittent bursts from the Tommy gun, adjusting his angle to ensure his targets were still at bay until the cops exited the lobby. When they were out completely, he moved again a little further to search for the Villalobos Brothers' thugs but they had disappeared. He raced up the stairs and stopped just inside the stairwell. The green fog permeated even here but it was dissipating, and with its passing Storm knew he would be easier to spot. He had only brought one of the smoke-grenades, so he'd had to make the difficult decision of when to use it; he had chosen to use it to get the cops to safety, and now he was out. He smiled grimly at the tension and the thrill of the chaos and adventure: he had many more tricks up his sleeves. Storm yanked his goggles off and began sprinting up the stairs.

A shot rang out from above, and Storm leaped back into cover just as a bullet splintered the wooden handrail before him. Just before the shot he had seen one of the gunmen lean down from the third-story landing while the other disappeared up the stairs to the next level. Flattened against the wall, Storm could hear the running of the shooter's feet above as he hurried to join his companion. He resumed his race up the stairs, stopping and peering around the corner of the third-floor hallway. He saw his two quarries escaping down the hall with Tolliver. Suddenly, as if he sensed the adventurer's eyes upon him, the second gunman turned and fired another shot. Storm ducked back as a bullet whizzed past him to smack into the stairway wall. He heard the feet of the shooter resume running, and knew he had to get past this thug in order to catch up with Tolliver and his captor.

Storm frequently wore a unique utility harness over his shirt. It was worn around his waist and over his shoulders and chest like a belt and suspenders. This harness housed many pouches for the unique tools and gadgets that he and his MARDL scientists designed for use in his adventures. From a pouch in his this harness he pulled a golf ball-sized steel sphere. Thumbing open a catch on the ball, he threw it toward the running man's ankles. The metallic ball spun as it flew, and cords with weighted ends unraveled themselves from their housing on the sphere. The cords of the bolo glistened: they were covered with some kind of strange chemical gel. When the bolo reached its target and the cords wrapped around the thug's ankles, not only did the bolo tangle his feet together but the chemicals on the cords reacted with each other to produce an instant, sizzling acid.

The running thug fell, yelling in pain and disbelief as his pant-legs smoldered and the acidic strands began to bite into his flesh. He dropped his gun hurriedly and began trying to untangle himself from the vicious device. He became more panicked when the acidic chemicals began to eat into the skin his fingertips.

Storm raced down the hall, kicking the pistol away from the man's reach... but he hadn't counted on the man momentarily forgetting his ankles and reaching out to grab one of his own.

Taken by surprise, Clifton Storm fell, but only for a moment. Twisting, he lashed out with his free foot and kicked the prone assailant hard in the face. There was a wet snap of a sound and the thug's head thumped to the floor, dead.

Freeing himself from the dead man's grip, Storm rolled and sprang to his feet. He had lost several precious seconds, and could feel Tolliver and his captor gaining ground ahead. He had to stop them before they got outside the hotel and away.

The man who had taken Tolliver hostage was sweating, and it wasn't from the exertion of the chase alone: things were not going as they had been planned. His only hope now was to get out of the hotel with his captive, who was being less than helpful and continued struggling to get away, despite the threats he was given. The thug wanted to knock him out, but knew carrying Tolliver's dead weight would make him move even slower.

The pair passed a street-facing window and the gunman froze with widened eyes. Down in the street, police cars were pulling up in droves while blue-uniformed cops swarmed toward the hotel. The thug cursed. Going down would not be an option now; between Challenger Storm's pursuit and the incoming police he knew he'd be out-gunned. Plus there was Skids to worry about: Storm's ally was still in the hotel somewhere. If the thug's comrade hadn't been successful in dealing with him, then he'd have to watch out for him as well.

The Villalobos Brothers' man's only hope now was the roof. Maybe he could get to it and jump with his captive to the top of the neighboring building. They were equal in height and close together on the Northern side of the hotel, and if he could persuade the older man to make the jump then maybe he could evade the police and Storm and get away with his captive.

"C'mon," he growled to his hostage, lightly rapping the top of his skull with the barrel of his pistol for good measure. "We're going up."

He dragged the tycoon with him hurriedly to the stairs and as silently as possible went up, past the fifth floor, up the final stairs to the roof access door at the top of the stairwell. He stopped for a moment to look up toward the door; it was dark here as the light fixture was out. He started up the steps when suddenly a small form leapt from the darkness, tackling him at the knees. It was Skids.

The three men rolled in a tumbling flurry of fists and oaths down the flight of steps and to the landing below. The Villalobos thug managed to climb over Tolliver to grapple with Skids, and once he got a free hand he struck the pilot a stunning blow to the chin. As Skids weakened, the criminal got to his feet and drew aim on Skids' forehead with his pistol, grinning wickedly. "So long, you little nuisance!" His trigger finger began to tighten…

A burst of Tommy gun fire echoed off the stairwell walls, and the killer's right shoulder was shredded by a hail of bullets. He shouted and dropped his pistol, sagging for a moment, and he saw the charging figure of Clifton Storm racing up the stairs.

Burning in the eyes of the troubleshooter was a look of anger unlike any the thug had ever glimpsed before, and the blue-grey eyes shone like menacing diamonds as Storm advanced toward him. Spurred toward sudden action by the terrible wrath that was approaching him, the gunman kicked the forms of Tolliver and Skids down the stairs toward Storm, then turned and scrambled for the roof door. He collided with it and broke it open, even as Storm nimbly leapt over the inert forms of Skids and Tolliver as they rolled down the steps toward him. In another moment, Storm was out through the access door and outside on the roof.

He caught sight of the Villalobos kidnapper just as he jumped from the roof of the hotel and onto the neighboring building. But the crook was in a panicked state and weak from the loss of blood from his bullet-riddled shoulder. His jump was easily completed but it was ill-timed, and he slipped as he landed. He grabbed onto the roof-ledge with his good hand, but was dangling, slipping.

Storm leaped easily onto the next-door roof and stooped down, grabbing the man's hand with both of his own. The thug dangled, trying desperately to get a footing on the bricks where he hung.

"Try to give me your other hand," Storm told him as he struggled to lift him up. Storm's physique packed a lot of strength into his trim frame, so strength was not a problem. The man's hand was slick with sweat, however, and he was slipping, sliding from the adventurer's grasp. The dangling kidnapper tried to reach up with his other hand, but he couldn't do it with his shredded shoulder muscles. He looked up into Storm's eyes for a brief moment, and then gasped as his hand finally slipped free.

The thug plummeted down five stories, limbs flailing in vain for purchase the whole time. It seemed to Storm as though he was watching a film going in slow-motion, and minutes seemed to pass before the man struck the alley pavement below with his head. He lay still there, twisted and broken in a widening pool of scarlet.

Storm bitterly stood up: although it was a necessity to sometimes take lives in his life's work, he didn't relish it, even if it was someone like the kidnapping vermin who tried to take Tolliver by force. He also knew that this man died taking secrets with him. He knew of one other member of the Villalobos' crew of thugs that was dead, and would soon find out that the others had died too at the hands of Skids. If they were dead, then none of them would tell them any information now.

Storm met Skids and Tolliver on the roof of the hotel; Skids confirmed the deaths of the other two Villalobos thugs to his boss as the troubleshooters saw to Tolliver's first aid. Apart from a few bruises, the businessman was in good health, and the three of them went down the stairs after calling to the police below that the situation was over. Besides the police, the incident had drawn crowds and reporters were now showing up as well. When word spread that Challenger Storm and one of his men were involved, the crowds began to grow. The two troubleshooters and Tolliver would have to avoid civilians at all costs to make a quick getaway: they had to get on with their departure to La Isla de Sangre, and soon.

"How'd you know to come here, boss?" asked Skids as they descended the stairs.

"I got a tip from a friend of mine on the Miami police department," Storm explained. "As you know, that group of guys that was after Mr. Tolliver last night was behind bars and not talking. All of a sudden, another guy showed up out of nowhere today with a lot of money and a slick-talking lawyer on the phone and demanded they be set free. Through some legal footwork, the fourth man sprung the others from jail. My informant got wind of it and knew we were working on a case for their intended target, so he called me and warned me that they were out. The two of you had already left for the hotel by the time I got the call and I figured they'd be going back to wait for Tolliver to show up and get his things."

A group of policemen were waiting for the men in the fifth floor hallway. As Storm approached them a swarm of questions greeted him. Under his breath, he said to Skids: "Now comes the fun part."

INTERMISSION ONE

The shining steel train was called the *Zephyr*, and it left the station in Washington, DC, amid a misty rain. Passengers settled in for their trip and began gazing from their windows as the passing scenery began whipping by at ever-increasing speeds. It had been grey all day. From a slate-colored morning through the foggy afternoon it stayed overcast, cold and damp to the core, and this seemed to fill the air with a certain sense of melancholy that the passengers were all too happy to see brightened by the warm light and richly-colored interior of the *Zephyr*.

In a private compartment onboard the train, a passenger settled in with a cup of coffee and some pastries. He had made sure the door was securely locked and that the interior window shades were drawn to block out the eyes of any passerby that strolled past his compartment. He didn't bother to draw the shades to the outside scenery. The passenger enjoyed long travel, and felt that it brought with it a feeling of calm and deep meditation. The man was blond and in his mid-thirties, and his suit was a somber and spotless jet black, offset by the loud mint-green color of his tie. He watched the grey rolling scenery outside as he enjoyed his repast, deep in thought about his assignment.

He had been called to the office of his superior the day before and had been tossed a dossier by the man behind the big oak desk.

"Have you heard of him?" the man across the desk had asked, folding his hands before him.

The passenger had nodded once he had seen the name typed on the file's index tab. "Sure. Who hasn't?"

"That's my point exactly, which is why we have to act now," his superior had said in reply. And then he went on to discuss what the passenger was to do. The passenger had listened, intrigued, but not without surprise. He had had a feeling for some time that his employers were going to take this

44

course of action eventually, he just didn't know that he was going to be the catalyst, the liaison and conduit through which their plans would come to fruition.

After the briefing, the passenger had gone home to pack for the next day, but had not read the files he had been given yet. There would be plenty of time during the trip for that…

As the passenger finished the last bite of his final donut, he wiped his mouth and sighed. The time was now for him to become better acquainted with the target of his employers' attentions.

He undid the clasp on the dossier, removed a packet from inside the outer folder and carefully broke the wax seal upon the envelope. He began to read the files within.

As the miles and the words wore on, he began to synthesize the information. Raw facts, news-clippings, private files, interviews and conjectures… all began to pile up like so much sediment. The words wove together into a history for the passenger, and as he read on he came to know the subject as though through a biography, a documentary film that played inside his mind as he went into a semi-trance…

Clifton Storm had been born wealthy, and it was a fact that he had always seemed to be aware of. Even as a young child, should he chance to be in a position to see other children who were of lower-income families, he knew and enjoyed the fact that he and his parents would have more than the others probably ever would.

He reveled in it. While his loving parents gave to various charities and causes that they supported, their young and only child mentally sneered at the poor, at the lower and unwashed people he saw as being beneath him and his aristocratic upbringing. "Why should our wealth be shared with anybody of such a low class?" he often wondered. "What makes those cretins so special that they need to leech off of my family's fortune?" His parents' charity and selflessness made him sick, and as good and kind as his mother and father were, young Clifton Storm was just as cruel and selfish.

While Gerald and Margaret Storm tried to instill honor and kindness and charity in their young son, it simply wasn't enough. His father was always busy running the vast steel company that was the source of the Storms' almost limitless wealth, and he was scarcely home. Because of this, consistent fatherly guidance was in short supply, and there seemed to be never enough time for the elder Storm to teach his son the virtues that he had learned in life.

His mother, too, had doted on young Clifton, but often just let the child have carte blanche over any chores or responsibilities. The family's staff of servants waited upon him hand and foot, and the young Storm got a perverse thrill from ordering these "lesser creatures" around.

All in all, the Storms had had noble intentions for their child, but lacked the discipline and attentiveness to make their values stick to his personality. Add to that Clifton Storm's exposure to his elitist schoolmates during his days at his private schools, and his values became twisted even further. Meanwhile, he had exhibited a high capacity for learning at school as well, but his laziness prevented him from using this potential to its fullest.

When Gerald Storm finally retired from his steel business, the tycoon had hoped that his increased free time would allow him to be closer to his family and that perhaps his influence could begin to affect his now callous and shallow son. By then, however, the damage had been done, and the surly and snobbish child had grown into a young man with worsened levels of the same traits, and who carried his trim frame with the same arrogance that blazed in his cold blue-grey eyes.

Determined to see Clifton do something with his life other than become a member of the idle rich, Gerald Storm set for his son an ultimatum: the now 19-year-old would either attend college so that he would be forced to make his own way in the world, or he would be cut off from the substantial family wealth. This created an argument of epic proportions between the Storms (who by this point had realized what their lack of attentiveness had created) and their son (who had resented the fact that he was now expected to actually *work* for something, which he'd never had to do before in his life). In rage and bitterness, Clifton Storm finally relented, his stubborn-brat mentality giving way to the knowledge that this course was one he would have to take to ensure that his high-society lifestyle would continue in the future.

The next day, Storm applied for the next semester at a prestigious college near the family home in upstate Michigan. A few days after that, still fueled by his bitterness and resentment, he set out alone on a private trip to Miami, Florida.

Ever since visiting the city with his parents as a boy, Miami had held an attraction for the young Clifton Storm. The "Casablanca of America" seemed to straddle the line between two worlds: one foot in the United

States and one foot in the exotic Latin countries, glamorous yet shady and dangerous, civilized in its cosmopolitan and urban way and yet primal as it reached into the swamps of the Everglades. The city drew Storm to it, and he often had made trips there as an adult, usually in the company of his few friends who found the tropical atmosphere conducive to their lifestyles of debauchery.

This time, however, Storm was traveling alone. After leaving the airport upon arrival, he had hailed a cab to the Biltmore hotel in nearby Coral Gables. Once settled at the luxurious hotel, he had bathed and changed into his evening attire, and after carefully concealing the bottle of illegal liquor he'd brought with him from Michigan, he had gone out.

He then spent the evening at various nightclubs with old friends, and the liquor flowed more and more as the night wore on… Storm had learned from previous trips where to get illegally smuggled or bootleg alcohol, and those sources didn't fail him. By the end of the evening, he had found himself in a very drunken state and without his local friends, but with a petite and equally tipsy blonde flapper by his side. Soon the pair had ended up at the ultra-exclusive Mortimer Club. Although his parents never frequented the social club because they looked down upon its policies of anti-Semitic "restriction," Storm didn't care about such topics and was able to get inside with his well-known family name on more than one occasion. After dining together at the Mortimer, Storm and the blonde had soon found themselves back at the Biltmore.

Shortly after the pair had arrived at Storm's room, there was a discreet knock upon the door. The hotel manager's rapping had been answered with a drunken "Go away," and a stifled feminine giggle.

The manager had adjusted his tie nervously and knocked again.

"I said go away!" came the slurred voice again.

The manager had cleared his throat. "I can't, sir. I have an urgent telegram for you, and I'm not to leave the door until it's delivered to your hand."

A muted curse had sounded from behind the closed door. The hotel manager had cleared his throat again. There was the sound of movement inside the hotel suite, followed by a stumbling sound and another high-pitched and drunken giggle…

The door then was yanked open. The smooth and handsome face that confronted the mousy hotel manager flashed cold and flinty blue-grey eyes, glazed by alcohol but nevertheless withering in their anger.

"This had better be important," Storm had growled to the shorter man. Behind him, the blonde was smoothing her flapper dress and stumbling.

"It is important," the manager had said as he handed Storm the telegram. "I'm very sorry, sir." He had bowed then and turned and strode down the corridor.

Storm unfolded and read the telegram, then froze. He read it a second time, then a third. Time stood still, and it seemed like an eternity before the girl's voice finally came to him as she called him across the room.

"What is it, Cliff?"

His tongue had seemed to be made of sand. "It's… nothing," he had said finally, laying the message down on the table. Then, without looking at her, he said: "Get dressed. I'm calling you a cab." He passed her and crossed the suite to the washroom and shut the door. The sink began to run inside the washroom.

The girl, her curiosity piqued, strode silently over to the telegram on the table. She picked it up, and then gasped as she read it:

RETURN HOME IMMEDIATELY STOP PARENTS KILLED IN
MOTORCAR ACCIDENT STOP MY CONDOLENCES STOP
ARTHUR M FRYE ATTORNEY

CHAPTER 6:
SUSPICIONS AND
DEPARTURE

There were many members of the Miami police department who were suspicious of Clifton Storm and his troubleshooting agency, but there were just as many admirers on the force as well. Once word had spread of his timely arrival and rescue of the two pinned-down cops in the hotel lobby, Storm had been gaining popularity among the cops on the scene; many of them who were there swore to him that they would stick up for the freelancer should his motives and reputation ever come under scrutiny.

After arranging to pay for the damages to the hotel, Storm and his companions snuck out of one of the hotel's side exits and hailed a cab; the MARDL fleet car that Skids had driven there would have to be picked up later by other members of the compound's personnel while their cab ride back to base would be more inconspicuous for the time being. After seeing Tolliver and Skids off in the taxi, Storm then phoned Marie from the hotel and arranged for statement to be arranged for the press, who had already begun phoning the MARDL compound the moment word of Storm's involvement got out. After this call, he walked his Harley-Davidson motorcycle out of the back exit and drove it down side-streets, avoiding the crowds of gawkers and eventually getting onto the open road that led to the MARDL facility.

The Miami Aerodrome complex was busy as preparations had already been ordered for the team's departure to La Isla de Sangre. Once he arrived, Storm went at once to the main hangar to supervise and assist with the loading of the gear. He was shortly followed by Tolliver, who had cleaned up and now silently watched the preparations from the sidelines. He appeared helpless and defeated as he stood and looked on.

Willy Avis observed the tycoon from across the hangar. In the Great War he'd served in the Army's 369th Infantry Regiment, also known as the Harlem Hellfighters, and had seen more action and bloodshed than a lot of Storm's crew. He recognized bad nerves when he saw them, and Tolliver seemed to have bad nerves to spare. The businessman was rich and not used to all the action he had found himself in, and Willy wondered how he was holding up. Deciding to gauge the fellow's state of mind, he walked over and casually introduced himself.

Tolliver shook his hand. Around them in the main hangar were aircraft of various size and purpose; some of the planes seemed to be unchanged, others slightly modified to serve Storm and his team's purposes. "This is a fine set-up you gentlemen have here," he said to the mechanic, looking around the spacious hangar.

Willy smiled. "Thank you, Mr. Tolliver. That means a lot coming from someone like you. Tell me: how are things at White Heron these days?"

Tolliver seemed to wince inwardly at the mention of his aviation company. "Business has been looking up lately. We have a few projects in the works that will change the way people fly... At least, that's what our official press says," he smiled.

Willy laughed. "Any hints you could drop?" he asked with genuine interest.

"Not at this time. Trade secrets, you know?"

He nodded. "I understand. The Valkyrie bombers, though... I'm sorry we never got to see those in production; all the talk about them said they were really supposed to be something special. Pardon my asking, but it is true that the government pulled your funding?"

"Actually, no; they asked for new designs to be produced..." Tolliver's voice trailed off, as if he'd caught himself mentioning something he shouldn't have and was unsure how to exit the situation gracefully. "Well, nothing's set in stone yet," he went on. "There are a lot of details that have to be worked out, especially after I return from La Isla de Sangre. Now then, Mr. Avis... if you'll excuse me, I have to retrieve a few things I'll need for the trip."

Tolliver started to walk away, but Willy stopped him with a hand on his upper arm.

"Mr. Tolliver…"

The magnate looked at the other man with sad eyes.

"Don't worry: we'll find Kate. We'll get her back safe."

Tolliver looked down again with a grim smile then turned away. Willy watched him go thoughtfully, then stepped out from the hangar and lit a cigarette. A few moments later, Clifton Storm reappeared carrying an equipment box. Willy motioned him out of the hangar to stand beside him.

"What's up?" he asked the mechanic.

"Cliff…" began Willy. "What do you think about Mr. Tolliver? You think he's being a hundred percent on the level with us?"

"The old man?" Storm asked. "You don't trust him?"

"'Old'? You know he's only a few years older than me, don't you?"

"Whoops, sorry." Storm grinned.

"You said that on purpose, didn't you?" Willy smiled back. "And no, I don't trust him. Have you noticed the lack of eye-contact when he speaks to you about certain things?"

Storm nodded, looking at Tolliver in the distance. "I have. And looking over his biographical details, I can't help but think that he's definitely not the shy kind of person."

Willy nodded. "He's got something to hide. It may not be much, but there's an angle we haven't been told about yet." Willy flicked cigarette ashes away, deep in thought.

"I got the same feeling," Storm agreed. "I had Marie do a follow up earlier. She contacted some American pressmen covering the strife in La Isla de Sangre. The abduction of Kate Tolliver by the Villalobos Brothers is big news there, and the community she was working with last has been up in arms for quite a while after her abduction; she's a saint to those people there. Her father's cause is legit…"

"So why'd he wait so long to bring us in? Why isn't he just champing at the bit to go get her?"

Storm wiped the sweat from his forehead with the back of his hand. "Good questions, Willy. I suppose we'll find out… probably the hard way."

Willy dropped his cigarette and chuckled. "Is there any other way?"

"Nope," Storm said with a smile as he watched Willy grind the smoking butt into the ground with his shoe. "Not for us."

The equipment was loaded, the fuel tanks were filled, and the Ford tri-motor was brought to the runway. It was the same red-and-silver plane that

"..Storm reappeared carrying an equipment box."

was used in the *Goliath* rescue. On the plane's nose beneath the cockpit's side window reclined a painted girl in a sarong, her bare back to the viewer and her face turned into the wind. Her hair and the flowers on the sarong around her hips were the same shade of crimson that adorned the plane. Next to her was the aircraft's name: the *Seeing Red*.

Storm, Willy, Skids, and Brock climbed aboard the plane along with J. Gordon Tolliver. The MARDL technicians waved farewell from the hangars while Marie stood and watched near the main office. Next to her, sad-eyed Buddy the dog watched the airplane. While Storm was away, Marie always took care of Buddy… or as she called him: "that ugly dog." This was a façade, though; deep down she liked Buddy, and the dog felt the same of Marie.

Once clear, the *Seeing Red's* engines roared to life. It taxied to the runways, and then gradually built in speed until it leaped off the tarmac. The tri-motor soared upward then banked and headed into the sky toward the south, the sun glinting off its metallic hide before it disappeared from view.

The journey was long, but the MARDL craft was outfitted for the long voyage. Even with the additional gas storage, however, they had to refuel the modified tri-motor often. Out of this necessity, their path zigzagged between airfields and friendly outposts along the way.

Between these stops, endless miles of sparkling sea and verdant jungle rushed by beneath the *Seeing Red's* wings. Their flight path carried them first to Havana, Cuba… a relatively short hop by aircraft from Miami. From Cuba, they headed across the sparkling Caribbean Sea to Honduras, then southeast to Panama. After their stop in Panama, another short flight brought them to Colombia, then Southwest to Ecuador. Finally, their course brought them exactly west along the equator to the Galapagos Islands, then past those tiny jewels of land…

It had been over 24 hour's total flying time since the plane had left the MARDL compound behind in Florida, but they were traveling west and ever into a new time-zone. Storm, Willy, and Skids had piloted the plane in shifts, resting and sleeping in turns. The trip was wearying to them, but they were set for the task at hand.

Any grogginess from the trip faded as beneath the sun the tiny, dark speck of La Isla de Sangre appeared on the horizon in the distance.

They had reached the Isle of Blood.

CHAPTER 7: CAPTIVE IN THE HOUSE OF WOLVES

The girl was in a roughly-constructed cell, an eight-foot by eight-foot cube of rough-cut timber and corrugated metal. In the center of the dirt floor, buried in a foundation of cement, was a steel pole that reached up to the ceiling of the shed where it was sturdily bolted into place. She knelt in the dirt next to the pole. Her hands were shackled, the length of chain between the cuffs passed through a loop bolted onto the pole near the floor. The chain was short, and her movements were severely restricted. She couldn't even stand up, much less stretch her limbs out very far.

Sunlight and fresh air struggled through the gaps between the wall and ceiling panels and beneath the sheet-metal door. The heat was stifling outside; in the cell that heat was magnified, nearly unbearable. Sweat rolled down her back, soaking her white blouse, her torn, dark skirt. Her head was down, her hair falling in a dark wing across her face. Her face could be considered beautiful in the outside world- it was oval and framed sparkling blue eyes and a generous, smile-ready mouth- but here, within the walls of the cell, it looked tired and ghostlike.

In her head, she kept seeing the soldiers, dressed in filthy drab fatigues, as they had stormed the one-room makeshift schoolhouse. There were three of them: one soldier had kept the children covered with his pistol as though they actually presented a threat to them, while the other two had grabbed her… but they had found a struggle. She had punched and clawed, kicked and bit at the soldiers, bloodying and bruising them until they had managed to strike her behind the ear with the butt of a pistol. Her head had lolled, dazed. From her stunned state of mind she had seen Hector, a normally quiet child in the front row, springing for the kidnappers. The third man had wheeled, knocking the boy back across a nearby desk, and then calmly drew aim and shot the boy where he lay sprawled across it. The other children had screamed and began panicking, and the soldier fired his pistol into the ceiling, silencing them to all but fearful whimpers as they had dragged her away.

The remembrance of that day left her nauseous and feeling helpless. In the cell, she now closed her eyes and thought of the children, of poor, brave Hector. She thought about the fact that she might not get out of this place alive.

It wasn't the first time she'd had this thought. And yet, she was still here, alive. She knew dangerous things, things about what the Villalobos Brothers were doing. Why was she still being kept alive?

A battered truck bounced along the dirt-road that wound through the jungle. In the truck was a pair of hardened-looking men; in the rear of the truck, a third man scanned the passing jungle foliage and the road behind them for any following trouble. Before this thug, an enormous machine gun sat on a tripod.

The truck rounded a corner and reached a fence and gate, beyond which sat the Villalobos compound: a sprawling collection of ramshackle huts and tin-roofed brick buildings.

After the gate's sentries inspected the truck for unwanted stowaways, they opened the gate and waved the truck through. It drove slowly through the compound toward the largest building… the men in the truck were in no hurry to deliver their news.

A crude porch was built upon the front of the building, and beneath its shade sat a pair of men. They rose when the truck came to a stop before them and waited expectantly. The first of the pair was tall and thin and seemed unnaturally smooth-shaven apart from his neatly-trimmed mustache. His white linen suit and Panama hat were remarkably free from any trace of dust or the blood-hued clay that seemed to stain everything.

He carried a cane, the silver handle of which was carved into a snarling wolf's head.

The second man's appearance seemed to vary as much as possible from the first. Although they were of equal height he was of a thicker build, and he wore drab fatigues that seemed to bear all the soiling and wrinkling that the other man's outfit was lacking... plus his own and then some more. A filthy black beret perched atop his head, and a pair of pistols sat at his waist, their bandoliers of ammunition crossing his chest in an "X." His face was scarred and ugly, almost beastlike, and he wore a sneer that never seemed to go away.

Although they didn't look alike, the Villalobos Brothers had been born identical twins. Esteban was the dapper one, and his refinement contributed just as much as his brother Jorge's cruelty and debauchery did to provide the contrast in their appearance.

Standing before the Villalobos Brothers, the three men from the truck shifted their feet nervously.

"Well?" asked Esteban, his voice smooth and controlled.

The driver finally spoke. "There has been no sign of them. No word, not a single telegraph or telephone call. They have not returned to the island. It is as if they disappeared in Florida."

Esteban looked at Jorge. "Then they have been stopped, either by the police, or by the man Tolliver went to see... the one the Americans call 'Challenger'."

Jorge smirked. "If he comes back with Tolliver, we have no need to worry. He is a man who bleeds and dies as any of us."

"But what does he know? How much could Tolliver have told him?" Esteban was silent for a moment, then: "Why don't you gather your pets, Jorge?" This was met with a smile from his evil-looking brother. Esteban turned to the trio of soldiers from the truck.

"You three come with us. We need to have another talk with our lovely school-teacher."

Katherine Tolliver heard footsteps in the dirt outside the door. She knew from the angle of the sun that it wasn't feeding-time... something other than a plate of food was going to come through the door. A bright knot of fear formed in her stomach, and she instinctively drew back from the door as far as her shackles would allow. The door's locks scraped and it swung back to reveal the Villalobos Brothers, along with three of their flunkies. The thugs undid her manacles and hoisted her up onto her feet, and she yelped as her cramped leg-muscles burned with pain. The trio held her tightly.

Esteban stepped into the room, followed by Jorge. Kate realized that with Jorge were three leashed wolves. The animals had a haunted look in their eyes, a fear and wariness as well as a powerful beastly hunger. The animals' bodies were thin and ragged; the wolves were kept near starving and were beaten often by Jorge himself to hone their ferocity. She had heard them crying out pitifully the previous night as he took his baton to them…

"*Señorita* Tolliver," Esteban said, breaking the silence. "We hope your lodgings here have remained adequate?" He smiled, displaying perfect white teeth.

Katherine avoided his gaze, the knot of fear tightening inside her. "What do you want?" she asked him, her disgust plain and audible.

"We just want to talk to you," Esteban said patiently, as though to an unruly child.

"I've already told you: I don't know where he is or what he's doing. I haven't spoken to him in days." She kept her head down, eyes focused on the base of the pole, wishing she could will the whole scene to go away.

"We know, Miss Tolliver. What we want to know now is this…" He lifted her chin with his cane, until her eyes were forced to meet his. "Has your father ever spoken to anyone about *Diosa de la Muerte*?"

"The *Goddess of Death*?" she translated. "I've never heard of it before. What is it?" Mystery suddenly gripped her as well. *Goddess of Death*? Very menacing-sounding… but what was it? Why would her father be doing with something with a name like that? *Oh, daddy*, she thought, *what have you gotten yourself into?*

"Miss Tolliver," Esteban said, lowering his cane, "I implore you to think very hard and very carefully. A lot of things may depend on this. Has he ever mentioned speaking to anyone about the *Goddess*?" He examined his perfect fingernails idly.

"I told you," she said firmly, "he never mentioned it to me. I have no idea what it is or why he would ever discuss something with a name like that. And if I did… you know I wouldn't tell you." She added this last declaration with defiance, her disgust rising like bile. She despised these men, and wanted them to know on no uncertain terms that she would never cooperate with them, even if she could.

Sighing tiredly, Esteban closed his eyes and massaged the bridge of his nose as he made a vague gesture with his other hand. Jorge and his wolves left the cell without a sound, and Katherine sensed something had just shifted in her situation, something unpleasant.

"Miss Tolliver, I sincerely hope we can trust you on that... but I think it's time to show you what happens to those we cannot trust." Esteban jerked his head toward the door.

The three guards led Katherine outside, where the dusty air and blazing sunlight caused her to squint her eyes in pain. Behind them Esteban followed, dabbing at his brow with a silk handkerchief. "*Ay*, this heat," he complained, seemingly oblivious to the sweat-soaked misery of his prisoner. "It's as though the planet is headed right into the gates of hell, eh Miss Tolliver?"

Kate did not reply; she just thanked God for the small comfort of a breeze and the chance to stretch her legs.

However, the thoughts of relief of any kind vanished as she saw the pit at the center of the compound... the pit she was being led towards.

At the edge of the pit the guards and their master halted. Kate looked down into the pit. It was about twenty feet deep and approximately seventy-five feet across. It was empty, bare clay except for a few bushes and a few scattered white rocks and stones of various sizes. The sides were steeply angled and offered no hand-holds. At one side, a heavy door and its frame were mounted in a shed-like building that projected from the side of the pit, and this seemed to correspond with another shed at ground-level near the edge of the pit.

From another cell-shed at the other side of the pit, a pair of guards pulled a man kicking and screaming into the sunlight. He was scrawny and filthy, his white undershirt stained with blood and sweat. Frantically, he dug his bare heels into the ground as the pair of guards dragged him. Frantic cries of "No! No!" only served to alert more of the Villalobos' guerrilla clan to come and watch the spectacle that was unfolding. There was no sympathy from them, and as Kate watched a soldier put his lit cigarette out on the prisoner's bare shoulder. The soldier laughed boisterously at his cruel act, but the prisoner showed no reaction... his wide, staring eyes were riveted on the pit. A chill ran down Kate's spine.

At the edge of the pit, the guards paused to cut the ropes that bound the prisoner's hands behind his back. While they did this, Esteban explained to Kate: "That man was a former lieutenant in our little army. We discovered that he was secretly meeting with one of our rivals and giving them, shall we say, sensitive information regarding some of our activities? As you can see, we can no longer trust him and so must do what is necessary." He turned and waved his cane at the guards holding the prisoner across the pit.

Roughly, they pushed him from the rim of the hole. He tumbled roughly down the embankment, and his fall was broken slightly by the bushes at the bottom. He screamed as he fell, though, and the sound sharpened upon impact.

After a moment, he staggered to his feet, his arm at an awkward angle… broken. A spike of bone protruded from his forearm near his elbow. "*Mi brazo! Mi brazo!*" he screamed in pain.

Kate's eyes were suddenly attracted to the white rocks at the prisoner's feet. She blinked, her eyes widening. She suddenly realized that the scattered white lumps weren't rocks at all…

They were sun-bleached bones.

At the side of the pit, the tunnel door burst open, and Jorge's starving wolves surged forth with murderous, hungry intent in their eyes. The prisoner began trying to flee the beasts. He reached the wall of the pit and scrambled at it, furiously clawing at the dirt, trying to climb footholds and handholds that just weren't there. The guards above him laughed and taunted.

Kate turned away; she couldn't watch. Esteban, however, slapped her hard across the face. Grabbing her by the hair he roughly turned her back to face the pit, forcing her to the edge.

"*Mira, cerdo, o te corto los párpados!*" he screamed at her. "Watch, pig, or I'll cut your eyelids off!"

As tears streamed down her face, Kate was forced to watch as the man was finally overtaken by the wolves. He went down finally, a scream cut short by the wolf tearing at his throat. The starving beasts went hungrily to work on him and his struggles slowed, then ceased entirely.

Esteban pulled her hair again, this time forcing her to face him. "And now you see," the suave voice back again, "what happens to those we cannot trust." He pushed her into the guards nearby. "Now take her back to her cell. Maybe she'll make sure she remembers anything else the next time we ask her to."

Esteban smiled as the guards took her back to her cramped shack. He had a feeling Kate was telling the truth about what her father had and hadn't said about *Diosa De La Muerte*, but this had been insurance. Her feisty spirit had been an annoyance to him. Perhaps the display of violence she had witnessed would help break that spirit.

CHAPTER 8:
THE SEARCH BEGINS

"What a dump!"

Skids, who had been sleeping during the last leg and approach of their trip, rubbed his eyes wearily. He had just stepped down from the *Seeing Red's* doorway and into the roaring tropical heat and humidity; the feeling of being smothered by hot and wet blankets assaulted him and the others. Skids made a face as he gazed around at the "airstrip." The sight that met his eyes was a seemingly unbroken expanse of red clay with no asphalt runways to speak of, just markings painted on the ground. It was bordered in the distance by a tropical jungle, which wavered in the heat-haze rising from the ground. "They don't even have a control tower here?" he said, astounded at the shock of landing in such an undeveloped location.

Willy tapped Skids' arm and pointed in the opposite direction from where he had been looking. A ramshackle building was there, rough-blocked and dirty, and beside this a rickety-looking radio tower loomed above. Beyond those structures were a shoddy-looking fence and a couple of taxi cabs, their shabby drivers smoking and chatting between them. In the distance, through the ever-present heat-haze, the outline of a city could be seen.

Skids looked again at the strip's "tower." "What can they do with that shaky thing? Chart the landing pattern of paper airplanes?"

Brock swatted him on the back of his head. "Didn't your mother ever teach you that lesson 'if you can't say something nice then don't say anything at all'?"

Skids sneered at the bigger man. "How about you, you gorilla? Didn't your mother ever teach you to walk upright?" he shot back, and he aimed a kick at Brock's shin.

"Knock it off, children," chided Storm as he hopped from the tri-motor. "We've got a job to do here." He observed their surroundings for a moment then turned toward J. Gordon Tolliver, who climbed out behind him. "Well, Mr. Tolliver… we're here, and the ball's in your court now. Lead the way for us."

Uneasiness spread across the tycoon's face as he looked again upon the dusty environment of La Isla de Sangre. "Well, I guess after we get our things settled at the hotel we should visit Kate's fiancé, Richard. I haven't spoken to him since I snuck out of the country. Perhaps he's heard something since I left, a lead we can follow. I'm sure he's been listening, waiting for something, anything to come up." His face was sad and drawn as he looked to the city in the distance.

After gathering their luggage, they piled into a waiting taxi, which soon was chugging its way from the airstrip. The cab ride through the island's capital city of Templo Del Sol offered the men an up-close view of city life on the island. An odd jumble of adobe huts and wooden shacks met them first, and as they drove further inward these gave way to larger block-homes and buildings. There was litter everywhere in this city, and the poor and impoverished seemed to be on every corner. It was an old country, slowly giving up its out-dated ways to the trappings of the new world. Progress had come to the tiny island of La Isla de Sangre, but not without a price. Despite the taller structures and modern building materials that were seeping their way in, there was no disguising the impoverished nature of the island. The newer structures at the heart of the city only served to make the juxtaposition of squalor stand out further to the visitors.

The face that answered the door of the little house near the heart of the city was smooth and handsome. Katherine Tolliver's fiancé, Richard Stein, could have been a matinee idol had he been in motion pictures. The test pilot seemed shocked at the sight of Tolliver and his two companions, and his jaw dropped.

"My God, Mr. Tolliver! Come on, get inside quickly." He hurried Tolliver, Storm, and Willy into the bungalow, locking the front door behind them. After casting a quick glance through the curtains at the window, he followed them into his living room.

"Where have you been?" he asked the tycoon. "You dropped off the face of the island with no warning, no notice. I was beginning to worry that the Villalobos Brothers had captured you."

Tolliver sat down tiredly. "I went back to the states, Richard. I had to. It took me a while to shake their men, and then I laid low for a while. When I felt that I wasn't being shadowed any longer, I drove to Florida... I knew they'd be watching the airports. They caught up with me while I was looking for help, but they were stopped..." He waved his hand toward his friends. "Richard, this is Clifton Storm and Willy Avis."

Stein turned to them, almost seeming to notice them for the first time. He shook their hands firmly.

"I've heard about you, Mr. Storm," he said to the adventurer. "All the papers call you 'Challenger'."

Storm smiled back. "Yes they do, unfortunately. They like to inflate things a bit; it's an annoyance."

"They're here to find Kate, Richard," Tolliver said soberly. "They're here to stop the Villalobos Brothers."

Stein sat down and laughed bitterly. "Well, that's easier said than done, I'm afraid. No one knows where they're at. The location of their hideout is still unknown." Stein turned back to Storm. "I've been working with the police chief since Mr. Tolliver left; the chief's name is Panza. He's been working diligently on her case but so far nothing's been found, no trace of her has turned up at all. Kate may as well have been kidnapped by ghosts."

Storm stared fixedly at Stein. "Are you absolutely positive? Her kidnappers are obviously infamous here. Someone somewhere has to know. Any leads, no matter how small, would be a help to us. As of now, the search for her could be like the proverbial needle in a haystack."

Stein thought silently for a few moments, and then rose to his feet. "Well, I've been told that I would be notified if something comes up, but it has been a few days since I last checked in with Chief Panza," he said. "I'll call him again; maybe there's been a break in the case. Wait here, I'll be right back." Richard Stein left the room to make his telephone call, leaving Storm, Tolliver, and Willy alone in his front-room.

There were dozens of framed photographs on Richard Stein's walls, and Willy's attention was caught by one that showed Stein smiling, standing beside a battered and broken plane engine. In the photograph the propeller blades were bent and mangled, and Stein was resting his arm on one. He was dressed in flying gear and all around him and the wreckage of the plane was a vast field of pumpkins.

Willy lit a cigarette and motioned toward the picture. "That's from the Sparrow X-11 crash, right?" he asked Tolliver. "I heard the port engine fell right off over a pumpkin patch and Stein put her down right in the very same field."

"That's right," Tolliver smiled. "Richard refused to be checked out by the doctors until he had his picture taken with both the airplane and the engine." He chuckled.

While the two men continued their discussion about Stein's flying feats, Storm got up from his seat and examined some of the pictures more closely. Richard Stein was a prominent figure in aviation circles, and he had flown more than two dozen experimental aircraft in the last few years. Some, like the Sparrow X-11, had crashed in near-horrific situations, but Stein was possessed by a lucky streak that always seemed to protect him from harm. It was this lucky streak, and his ability to put all the aircraft that he flew though extremely rigorous test flights safely, that made him one of the top test pilots in the world and ensured that he stayed in that position. His career was spelled out in the pictures on his walls, and they projected a sense of the man. The photos showed him with the airplanes he flew, heads of aviation firms, and notable celebrities and figures in society…

Storm's reverie was interrupted by Stein's return to the living room. He grinned at his visitors. "Say, talk about having good timing!" he said. "Panza says they just received a tip within the hour that they haven't had a chance to act upon yet. It could lead right to the Villalobos conclave." He crossed his arms and leaned against the wall proudly. "I explained to Chief Panza that independent operators from the United States were involved. When I told him who it was, he told me that he wishes for Storm and his men to personally accompany a police expedition out to the site. This could be the big lead we've been looking for, and they're preparing for this search right as we speak."

Storm looked at Willy and nodded tersely, and then turned to Tolliver. Before he could say anything, however, Richard Stein interrupted him by speaking to the tycoon.

"Mr. Tolliver, while you're here, I need your help desperately with some information regarding a project that I've been invited to participate in back in the States. Will you stay here with me and give me some advice while your friends investigate?" He turned to Storm. "I'm sure between them and the police the situation will be well in hand."

"Okay, we probably won't need your help right this minute, Mr. Tolliver," Storm said to the mogul. "But I do think that as a matter of protection Willy should stay behind here. I want the two of you watched, just in case someone from the Villalobos' gang shows up." Willy nodded at this, and Storm knew that the mechanic was just as capable as the younger members of his group at handling any trouble that might spring up.

From Stein, Storm wrote down the directions to the police station as well as the test pilot's phone number; then, bidding the men goodbye, he left in their hired car for the hotel to pick up Brock and Skids, who would be accompanying him and the police team on the expedition.

The police station was only a small, four-story edifice, but it somehow seemed to tower over the immediately surrounding dwellings in the city due to its relative modernity of its design and construction. Inside, Storm, Brock, and Skids were met by Panza, the police chief. Thin and bearded and wearing a rumpled uniform, Panza seemed friendly and eager to help Storm and his associates.

"Ah, my friends," he said cordially as he shook their hands. "From what Mr. Stein told me, I was expecting there to be four of you. Well, it doesn't matter. Three should be sufficient as plenty of my men will be with you. It seems you have arrived on the island at a most opportune moment; ever since I took over from the previous chief of police I have hoped for the day that we would find a thread, some lead to help us find the Villalobos Brothers. At last, it seems we have found that lead." Panza closed the door to his office as Storm and Skids sat down, and then the chief himself sat down behind his desk. He regarded the troubleshooters with large curious eyes peering through his spectacles.

"We're glad to hear that there might be a break in the case," Storm asked. "I know from what we've been told that the Templo del Sol police have been working a long time on this. What happened to the previous chief of police? Was he unsuccessful in the investigation as well?"

Panza grimaced. "Very unsuccessful, although he did try his best to find them. Unfortunately, for his attempts he was hung from his ankles and had his throat slit, right in his very own home."

"Cute," said Skids.

Panza went on. "He may have gotten too close to the truth or perhaps he confided in someone that he shouldn't have... but for whatever reason, he was killed. Upon his death I was reassigned to Templo Del Sol from the other side of the island. With the reassignment came a promotion and the investigation is in my hands now."

"Yeah, lucky you," smirked Skids again, and Brock rolled his eyes at his friend's constant attempts at humor. "Don't you ever shut up?" the big man asked him in a whisper.

Panza ignored the exchange and got up from his desk. "And now, gentlemen... if you'll excuse me, I have to finish assembling the expedition you'll be traveling with." He bowed stiffly and left Storm and the other two alone.

"Guys," rumbled Brock quietly. "Someone's been watching us since we got here. I can see him from here where I'm standing."

The group remained nonchalant. Skids muttered "See Brock, now that's the advantage of being a big ape: you can see over the trees." He was silenced by Storm's elbow in his ribs.

"What's he doing now, Brock?" the scarred leader asked, pretending to examine his fingernails.

"He's still giving us the hairy eyeball." Brock then saw the man, thin and sharp-eyed, rise from his desk and began to come toward the office.

"I think he's coming over—"

Brock didn't finish. Panza had returned to the room with a tough-looking officer. "Gentlemen, please follow the sergeant here," he told them. "The expedition is about to leave. If, indeed, this is a Villalobos hideout that this tip leads you to, you will then return for the gathering of a full-scale raiding party." He grinned. "We'll get these outlaws yet."

Storm and his associates followed the sergeant, a man introduced as Lopez, down a hallway and to the rear of the station. There a pair of rugged trucks was waiting, and a party of twelve men had been assembled. Storm and his men climbed into the second truck.

The vehicles headed from the city, driving westward. The inner city gave way to the squalor on the outskirts, then the poorer sections of the city, then nothing. The roughly-paved road gradually gave way to a dusty dirt track, then eventually to worn grass trails; all the while the wild and dense jungle and its oppressively hot atmosphere seemed to close in on them. Conversation between Storm's men and the rough-looking police squad was nearly nonexistent, and they finally ceased conversation even amongst themselves as the grim drive wore on.

The trucks eventually turned off their grassy path and into the surrounding jungle, and they continued onwards through the thick growth. After bouncing through the foliage for an indeterminate period of time, the trucks finally braked to a stop.

Quietly, the vehicles emptied of their men. The police were armed with submachine guns, while the Americans had their pistols. Storm drew his Mauser from his utility harness; Brock brought his automatic from his shoulder-holster and Skids drew his Colt revolver from his gun-belt. Although the intent of this journey wasn't combat, the weapons were necessary in case trouble sprang up…

The line of men wove its way into the jungle, led by Sergeant Lopez, who consulted a map from time to time. The equatorial heat and stifling jungle humidity bore down on them like a heavy, wet blanket. The noises of the jungle seemed muted, as if even the animals and insects felt the oppression of the swelter as well. Sweat coursed down the men's bodies, and they had to stop a few times to drink from their canteens of water.

The slight noises of the jungle eventually gave way to the gentle roaring of the ocean; they were approaching a beach. The squad finally broke through the trees and before them was revealed a wide, white stretch of sand lapped by gently breaking seawater.

It was all a beautiful scene of the tropics, a postcard's view of paradise... but there was no warlord encampment here on the beach, only an unexpected scene: a deep pit had been dug into the sand, and a pair of unlit kerosene lanterns sat on the ground beside some shovels.

The line of men broke up, and Storm and his men advanced onto the beach toward the pit, confusion taking hold in their minds.

"It's been a wild goose-chase," Storm said. He holstered his pistol as Skids and Brock did the same.

"Must've been a bad lead?" asked Skids, scratching his head.

Storm regarded the pit before him, the possibilities racing through his head. Suddenly his instincts shrieked; he had a feeling like spiders walking on his spine as his almost extrasensory feelings of danger awoke.

"No... not a bad lead Skids..." he said, whirling around to face their escorts as the sound of weapons being cocked filled the air. "A set-up."

"A set up!"

CHAPTER 9:
TROPICAL NIGHTMARE

S torm's aides also spun to face their betrayers. The policemen stood on a slight rise in the terrain at the edge of the jungle where the grass met the sand, and their guns were held steady on the trio. Lopez lit a thin cigar and grinned around it. The scene on the beach had been lush and serene, and now it had become a ghoulish tableau as the adventurers found themselves under guns and on the spot.

"My friends," Lopez addressed them, "you are outsiders, and you must realize that outsiders have no place on La Isla de Sangre. There are certain rules to be followed here, and probing questions are just unwelcome. The world turns its eyes from us and pretends that we do not exist… and we prefer it that way." He blew a cloud of smoke. "We are hidden from your civility, and we don't care because we have no need for it." Then another puff and more smoke. "Now… put your hands up and line up along the pit, if you please."

The three captives were outnumbered and outgunned, and they did as they were told. Storm's mind raced; he needed some time to stall them. Katherine and J. Gordon Tolliver and Richard Stein- perhaps even all of the island's residents- were counting on them. The thought of him and his men dying here in a hidden corner of the world and perhaps never to be found touched his soul with ice.

"These 'certain rules' you mentioned," he said to Lopez as he raised his hands. "Would they include the kidnapping of innocent women? Or how about the killing of defenseless children, do they also include that?" At his back the pit yawned; their intended mass-grave awaited them.

Lopez looked at the adventurer steadily. "*Señor* Storm, the Villalobos Brothers are a part of the oldest known families here on the island. They can trace their family lineage all the way back to the native tribes that once dominated the island before the Spanish colonized it. All of La Isla de Sangre is their birthright, and they just want to have what's coming to them. And so, to use one of your country's expressions, you cannot make an omelet without breaking a few eggs." He grinned through a fresh cloud of cigar smoke as his compatriots laughed.

"Oh, yeah?" Skids chimed in. "Well, your omelet stinks like sh—"

"Shall we dispense with this delay now?" Lopez asked, cutting the pilot off. "Once we get back to Templo Del Sol, we've been told we can divide up your belongings amongst ourselves. For your deaths, I get your airplane. I have always wanted to fly." He smiled proudly.

Storm's forehead was beaded with cold sweat, adrenaline pumping through him. "Well, I hope you enjoy it, Lopez. Before you kill us, there's just one thing left for my men and I to do."

"And that is?" Lopez put his foot up on a rock, resting an elbow on his knee.

"Scatter!" Storm barked, and his foot lashed out. It caught the nearest oil lamp, launching it toward Lopez as though it was a kicked football. The crooked sergeant had no time to react.

The lamp smashed upon the impact with his face. The oil was ignited by his cigar, and it spread out to cover him and the two men at his sides in a fiery orange sheet. The three men were engulfed in flames, and Lopez ran in a blind panic. He tripped over the rock he'd been resting his foot upon and it pitched him forward, falling head first into the intended grave-pit. Scrambling in vain to get out of the pit, he was burned alive while the other two flaming men ran madly into the jungle. Screams of anguish ripped out into the early tropical evening.

The other ambushers, startled by the conflagration, had been too stunned to shoot the victims during the lightning-quick events; the three intended victims had scattered as Storm gave the command and scrambled into the jungle. Their would-be killers snapped out of their stunned haze and began firing at their targets in vain. The whining bullets kicked up only sand.

"After them!" someone screamed. "Don't let them escape!" The nine remaining killers scrambled after their chosen quarry.

The killers had lost their position of advantage over Storm and his men, and the odds were now evening.

A pair of gunmen raced into the jungle behind Brock. The former circus strongman was much faster than he appeared, and the duo had a hard time keeping up with him. To their right, a third comrade of theirs was spotted, and they called to him to follow.

The jungle ahead was getting denser and thicker, but they were following the disturbed foliage and the crashing sounds in the underbrush, not needing to see their huge quarry to be drawn to him.

Ahead, Brock suddenly entered into a brief clearing in the foliage. He spun around to face his pursuers and his automatic hammered twice. A pair of slugs found their mark and a gunman went down. The other two pursuers opened up with their submachine guns. A staccato song of death blared out toward the strongman, but Brock had already turned and continued his flight across the clearing and the shots went wide. The bullets struck a patch of foliage beside a large tree just as he dove into it and then all was still.

The pair of killers advanced cautiously, weapons ready. Moving into the thick brush, they pushed aside branches with the snouts of their guns. They found only tattered leaves... no body.

The first pursuer continued beyond the clearing and into the foliage. His companion lingered there by the tree for a moment...

A huge pair of hands shot down from the branches over his head. They swiftly drew the would-be attacker up, and the sound of his neck snapping was like the report of a rifle shot as his body went slack.

The first attacker spun at the sound, bringing his gun up to aim at Brock as he perched in the tree. The killer fired a burst, but his quarry had already brought his dead ally's body before him to use as a shield and the bullets impacted into the already dead form. From behind his improvised shield Brock fired his pistol twice more, and the gunner below went down like a rag-doll.

At that moment, Skids was running headlong into the jungle. Behind him were shouts as his pursuers streaked though the jungle after him. He vaulted over a fallen tree, trying as hard as he could to put distance between himself and the pair of men chasing him...

Suddenly, another crooked policeman stepped from behind a tree right in front of him, and Skids collided with him. They went down in a tangle of fists and curses. Then, a gunshot rang out...

The two pursuers came upon the scene several moments later. Just past the fallen tree, they saw their comrade. He lay still upon the ground, his blood pooling around him, soaking into the dark jungle soil. Skids' tracks ended at the scuffle. The pursuers swung their guns around, searching in vain. There was no sign of their intended victim.

While one of the gunmen stood guard, the other climbed back over the downed tree. Investigating the body of his comrade, he found the dead man's pistol missing. He straightened up…

There was a pile of leaves on the ground beneath the fallen tree; the leaves suddenly seemed to explode as an arm shot out of each side of the pile. In one hand was a massive revolver, in the other the dead man's automatic. The two pistols thundered as one, and on each side of the log a killer slumped down dead, death taking them before they even realized what had happened.

Skids climbed out from the pile of leaves under the arch of the fallen tree, dead leaves sticking out of his normally perfect hair.

"Isle of Blood," he said to no one, wiping sweat on his sleeve. "C'mon, Skids, it sounds like a great place, you'll love it." He spat.

Storm had pursuers to worry about as well. His white shirt stood out more plainly than the clothes that Skids and Brock had been wearing, and so he constantly sought out the deepest pockets of green and shadow as he tried to distance himself from his pursuers.

Sensing that he was out of sight but that his pursuers were near, he dove through a particularly thick patch of wild ferns then crouched and rolled into an equally thick growth to his right. Squatting there for tense seconds, his two adversaries ran past. Then… he sprang at the last man, tackling him. Tumbling over each other, they rolled down a small embankment.

The man gave a startled cry and managed to squirm out of Storm's hold, then raised a foot to kick at Storm as they were standing up. Storm caught the foot in mid-blow, however, and twisted it hard in his hands. A sickening scrunching sound came from the attacker as his ankle popped.

The policeman screamed from rage and pain, but yanked his useless foot away and managed to lunge at Storm rather than try to pull away. He knocked the adventurer off his feet, and the attacker then scrambled on top of him, wrapping his hands around Storm's throat.

Gasping for air, Storm drew back his arm and struck his opponent in a flat-handed jiu-kudo strike, jabbing the attacker's throat like a spear. The deadly fighting art, known by very few in the western world, turned the hands and feet of its practitioners into deadly, whistling instruments of death. The rigid fingers crushed the other man's windpipe. His attacker let go and gurgled in death as Storm got to his feet.

Suddenly, a chattering blast of submachine gun-fire erupted from above, bullets whizzing just inches from Storm's head. He dove to the ground, grabbing the killer's fallen weapon as he rolled, and fired it blindly up the embankment. His hasty shots were wide, missing the shooter there. Storm rapidly took cover behind a large tree.

Up on the slope, the shooter laughed roughly. Storm leaned out to try for a clearer shot, but a volley of his opponent's bullets forced him back behind the tree. "Damn it," he gritted under his breath and through clenched teeth. From behind his cover, he couldn't see his attacker, only the vine-covered tree behind the gunner. He considered using a luminous smoke-grenade to blind his attacker, but realized that the open air here could cause the cloud to dissipate, or that his target might change positions too quickly for Storm to put him into his sights. He had another plan.

He removed a small signal-mirror from his equipment harness and held it in front of him. From here he was able to gauge his attacker's position by using the mirror without exposing himself.

Storm turned and fired his procured submachine gun up the embankment at the tree. He waited a moment, checking his shots in the mirror, and then fired another burst, then another.

His attacker laughed. "*Señor* Storm, your shots are so wide. Why don't you come out of hiding so you can get a clear shot at me?" he taunted.

Storm fired up the little hill again, spending the last rounds from the gun's clip. He tossed it aside and drew his Mauser from its holster. He checked in the mirror again. "Clear shot?" he called back, and fired a round from the pistol. "I don't need a clear shot." A second shot. "Not at you, anyway." A third...

The massive branch he had been firing at suddenly tore loose with the third bullet from the Mauser. It fell and swung, held by the vines that were wrapped around it. The heavy limb cut a powerful arc through the air like a massive sledgehammer. The gunner turned his head just in time to see it heading for him, but was too late to move...

The huge limb smacked hard into the gunner amid the sound of snapping bones. Its momentum threw him through the air to land, twisted and still, amid the bushes ten feet away.

Storm arrived back on the beach a short time later. The sky was just starting to darken now and a breeze blew in off the ocean to cool the sweaty humidity, even if it was just for a temporary respite from the oppressive dampness. He removed the bullets from his pistol and loaded it with several of what his team referred to as "signal caps." These were bullet-like rounds of ammunition that fired no projectile but were specially designed to make a lot of noise. He kept a captured weapon trained on the trees just in case there were still killers lurking there, and he fired his specially-loaded Mauser several times, a series of shots in a pre-determined signaling sequence. In a few moments, returning sequences of shots came from the jungle, signifying the safety of his companions. Soon Brock and Skids emerged from the jungle, and the trio counted up their defeated opponents.

"Three of them were torched by that lantern trick," Skids said, looking at Lopez's smoldering corpse in the pit. "I got three of them myself."

"There were two after me that I know of." Storm turned to Brock.

"I took out the three that were after me," the third man said, rattling the weapons he'd taken from his opponents.

Storm looked to the way they came to the beach. Many footprints led to the sand from that path… but only one pair went back. "That leaves just one crooked cop left."

Fearing that one of the attackers had gotten away, they hurried back to the trucks. They found both vehicles exactly where they'd left them. Skids and Brock lifted the flap of the heavy canvas cover on the bed of each truck, prepared for an ambush by the missing member of the party. There was no ambush, however.

"Where the hell is this guy?" asked Skids, peering into the surrounding jungle.

"Here," Storm said.

He opened the cab in the second truck and the missing man's corpse fell out heavily, a revolver slipping from his dead fingers. A single, neat bullet-wound adorned his right temple.

"Geez," rumbled Brock. "Was he that scared of us?"

Storm bent over the body, exposing the dead man's chest. A stylized wolfs-head was tattooed over his heart. "No," he said, "he was scared of his bosses… the Villalobos Brothers."

"Failure's not an option to these people," said Skids.

Storm said nothing. He drew a length of hose from the truck and set about siphoning its remaining gas into the other one to ensure there would be enough fuel for the trip back to the city. A silence hung over the scene, eventually broken by the droning of heat-bugs.

Brock finally spoke: "This place is so corrupt... Think this has something to do with that shifty guy at the police station?"

Storm considered for a moment. "Maybe," he said. "Whoever set us up did so pretty well. In defending ourselves, we became the murderers of policemen. They may have been crooked cops, but they were cops just the same. Even though we won this fight, what happened here leaves us at a disadvantage. We're going to be hunted now... and we'll need to be careful." He thought for a moment, his mind turning behind his blue-grey eyes. "Let's get back to the city," he said finally. "We need to try to find these guerillas on our own, without the help of the locals... I just hope they haven't gotten to Willy, Tolliver, and Stein first."

Shortly thereafter, the lone truck trundled back to civilization as the sun finished setting. The rules had changed a little, now, and the players were going to have to learn to adapt.

CHAPTER 10:
DIOSA DE LA MUERTE

The Pantera Clan, whose ramshackle base of operations was based in the southern mountain range of La Isla de Sangre, were the first to feel the wrath of the *Goddess of Death*.

It was a clear, almost cool night now. Many members of the guerrilla group sat around a blazing fire in the center of the camp. It was supper-time, and they balanced tin-plates of chicken and beans on their laps. Tequila was passed around, and the sound of rough laughter and conversations rose into the night.

Raphael Contento, the leader of the Pantera Clan, stood in the doorway of one of the enclave's shacks and watched his men. Of the three rogue factions on the Isle of Blood, theirs was the smallest. However, as they had proven time and again, they were in no way the weakest. The Pantera Clan was made up of fierce, hardened fighters, and they would remain that way until their dying day.

Raphael sipped his cup of chicory and looked to the line of mountains to the west. Night had fallen not too long ago, and twilight framed the peaks of those hills, faintly outlining them against the sky. They were beautiful, those mountains; looking at them, Raphael could understand how so many legends had sprung up on this wild, rugged island. There was superstition among his people, grounded in the fearsome reputation that their ancestors had once had. The hills and valleys and jungles of La Isla de Sangre concealed many mysterious ruins, and these were shunned by the populace. As he gazed at the mountains while deep in thought about the island's shadowy history, he was startled as he thought he detected a faint purple glow above one of the peaks. However, when he blinked and focused his eyes, it was gone... probably a trick of the early starlight.

He turned to the dirty 18-year-old girl in the shack and demanded his cup be refilled. Her bruised and grimy face showed no emotion… it had stopped doing so some time ago, shortly after she had been kidnapped by the Pantera Clan. The only emotion she held now was hope… hope for her own death, as she knew these warlords would never let her go free.

As she bent to lift the pot of chicory from the small cooking fire Raphael leered at her. She filled his cup and turned away and he laughed harshly, and then left the shack. He stopped on his way to the fire, the cup of hot chicory halfway to his lips and the smile fading from his face. The purple glow was back above the mountains in the west, and it definitely was no trick of the twilight.

The others had seen it now too, and they stood. They watched the faint violet aura with fascination. The night was still now; a moment before there had been a faint droning sound but it had ended now, producing a vacuum of sound that even crickets dared not to disturb. The glow was passing some low clouds now, and it was reflected off of them.

The men on the ground squinted, trying vainly to gain an outline, some defining shape of the glow that could give it an explanation. What could be producing it? As it neared them, a sense of wonder filled the hardened and filthy criminal group.

Suddenly the air was filled with a tremendous roaring sound. The glow swooped down from its course, swinging in within the range of about 200 feet above the ground and then… its dive stopped abruptly.

The Pantera Clan grabbed for their guns as it hovered there, unsure of what the tumultuous sounding apparition was, as the roar was louder than ever now…

Suddenly, sweeping beams of light shot out from the ghostly, glowing shape that hovered above them. The lights blinded the guerrillas as they vainly began to fire their weapons upward toward it. The sense of wonder had turned to panic as the Pantera Clan confronted the menacing apparition.

It was then that hell broke loose from the sky.

Whistling tongues of flame streaked out from the thing. They raced down from the hovering glow, obliterating the Pantera Clan's vehicles in violent fireballs, while thin dotted streams of destruction swept the chaotic mass of men. Some ran from the wrathful thing in the sky, while a few brave souls stood their ground with their weapons or fired at it from behind cover… all were mangled, ripped full of holes or burned to a crisp, or simply blasted into nothingness by the onslaught.

Raphael Contento watched from behind an outcropping of rock as the thing from the sky massacred his men. His confusion and fear was at a fever-pitch as he witnessed the thing from the mountains slaughtering his men. It was a fierce, otherworldly power. In the midst of all this, he surprised himself by remembering the words of a prayer and was further surprised to find himself saying it out loud, although his voice was lost in the roaring chaos, a whisper in a thunderstorm.

The roving and lighted gaze of the demon in the sky was everywhere: whenever the cones of glaring light highlighted a figure on the ground, that figure would be annihilated. There seemed to be no escape. Unless...

Behind the rusty tin shacks, just on the other side of a hilly rise, there was a dusty and seldom-used road that wound away into the hills, where there was tons of caves and hiding places. If Raphael could make it to that over that rise, maybe he could get away from this thundering judgment that had come for the Pantera Clan. He felt ashamed and cowardly, but cared nothing for his swagger and pride now. His only thought and wants were of self-preservation.

He waited until the time was right, until the thing seemed to be looking the other way... then he bolted. He ran between the shacks, legs pumping and chest burning with the exertion of his flight and the single greatest fear he'd ever known. At any moment he expected to be lit up by the gaze of the thing, to feel his body ripped to shreds. He was closer now to the ridge. He pushed on. He was up the rise, now, feeling horribly naked and exposed. He raced on, ever-expectant of the white light, the death and fire that followed it...

And then he was over the crest, tripping on an exposed root and falling, rolling over and over until he came to a stop next to the road. It was not a graceful exit, but he had made it. Battered and bleeding, but away from the destruction that was still filling the air with thunder and screams, Raphael Contento was alive.

He crawled beneath a small patch of scrub brush and waited. The chaos and bloodshed eventually slowed and ceased, but the roaring noise continued. Whatever was hovering over the smoking ruins and carnage was searching, looking for survivors.

Suddenly, the roaring intensified and changed pitch. Raphael took a chance and poked his head from under the bushes and looked past the rise he'd fallen down.

The apparition was leaving, rising straight up into the air. It's searching beams were gone now, and again the gentle violet glow could be seen disappearing into the night as the tremendous roaring faded. Soon, it was just a faint spot in the distance, and then nothing else remained of it.

Shakily, Raphael got to his feet. He was unsure now of what to do. Was he the last member of the Pantera Clan left alive? He began to climb the slope he'd fallen down previously. His ears were ringing, but beyond that sound he thought he heard something else... the drone of engines? He continued his climb, fear again taking hold.

At the top, he paused and peered over the ridge.

Three trucks had rolled into the ruins of the Pantera Clan's hideout. Men were swarming now about the bodies, searching for weapons and belongings. They were looting what was left of the clan of rebels and sudden indignity took hold inside of Raphael. Who were these men, and what was that thing in the sky that had murdered his men?

Moving furtively, he skirted the remains of the shacks and buildings that had once been his domain. His pistol was in his hand, although he knew he'd never be able to take all of them on. His thoughts raced and his blood boiled in rage. What should he do?

He wouldn't get a chance to do anything.

A gun muzzle pressed into the back of his neck, and a voice commanded him to drop the gun. Raphael let the pistol, heavy suddenly, fall from his hand.

"*Oye!*" his unseen captor called to his compatriots. "Hey!"

Fatigue-clad roughnecks began to appear now and circle around the captor and his hostage. Some of them recognized Raphael, and raucous taunting began to surround him, stabbing his pride.

With desperation, Raphael spun around and tried to snatch the pistol from his warder. He failed. The hostage-taker, a youngish-looking soldier with a cruel line of a mouth, swung his weapon in a back-handed strike. The impact of the steel caused Raphael to stagger backwards, stunned. Another soldier stepped in, viciously kicking the Pantera Clan's leader in the stomach. He doubled over in agonizing pain, and yet another kicked him in the right knee. Raphael went down in a heap, preparing to be beaten to death as the circle of men closed in on him.

They stopped as someone shouted an order, and then silence fell. The group parted, and through blurry eyes Raphael could see a filthy pair of combat boots walking toward his prone form... along with several pairs of furry legs. He looked up.

Jorge Villalobos and his three leashed wolves looked down on him murderously. "*Hola*, Raphael," he greeted him icily.

Raphael hung his head as he struggled to his hands and knees. He felt a horrible shame: he had been bested by the Villalobos Brothers here on his own turf. That thing from the sky had decimated his clan in a matter of minutes, and they had swooped in afterwards to reap what they could scavenge from the remains of his once proud group of soldiers.

And now he was their final prize, as leader of the Pantera Clan.

"So, what is he to us now?" asked the cruel and youthful fighter who had caught Raphael originally.

"Prisoner?" another soldier asked. Another said, "Buzzard meat?"

"No," answered Jorge, still looking down at his captive. He grinned, his teeth decayed and fang-like, while his wolves licked their lips and panted.

"No," Jorge repeated. "He's dog food."

Raphael Contento surprised himself again and resumed praying frantically as Jorge moved to unleash his pets.

CHAPTER 11:
A NEW ALLY

Templo Del Sol would now be an unfriendly place. Clifton Storm and his companions had killed corrupt policemen. True, they had been on the Villalobos Brother's side and payroll, and it was done in self-defense… but they had killed members of the police force nonetheless. The troubleshooters would have to leave the capitol city immediately and would have to relocate to another site from which to continue their search… a search that was still without any leads. The authorities and law-enforcement departments here were rife with corruption as had previously been expected, and so they were now to be avoided entirely.

And so it was with a shock that Storm, Brock, and Skids returned to Richard Stein's bungalow and found a detective- the same thin and keen-eyed man who had been observing them at the police station. He was sitting with Willy, Stein, and Tolliver in the bungalow's living room. The detective rose when Storm and his men entered, but before he could address them Brock stepped forward threateningly. The giant gripped the thin cop by his coat lapels and hoisted him up against the wall, despite Tolliver's shout to wait. The detective found the crown of his hat crushed against the ceiling and angry eyes burning before his own.

"Brock!" Storm's voice cracked out like a rifle shot in the little house.

"Cliff, this is the guy that was givin' us the stink-eye in the police station," the big man growled. The normally placid Brock was seething with rage at the suspected source of their betrayal and attempted murder by the police.

"Friend," Storm addressed the hoisted fellow, "we've just been through hell and you're one of our prime suspects… we'd like an explanation about what's going on and we'd like it now. Do you want to start talking?"

"Hhkk…" the reddening detective gurgled out, strangling.

"Let him down, Brock," Storm said. "He can't breathe."

The bald strongman lowered his captive and loosened his hold on the man's clothes, but still held fast to his coat.

Breathing deeply and rubbing his throat, the man began:

"My name is Anando Del Rio. I'm head investigator of Templo Del Sol's police department, and in charge of tracking the movements of the Villalobos Brothers… that is, I used to be in charge of it." He looked at Storm with bleary eyes. "Water, please?"

Tolliver had risen from his chair along with the other men during the scuffle, and he now fetched Del Rio's glass of water from the table near where he'd been sitting. The detective swallowed greedily, the water easing the pain in his throat. When he had drained the glass, he resumed:

"The pursuit of the Villalobos Brothers, as well as their rivals the Pantera Clan and Cráneos Del Infierno… that was my job. It became an obsession to me, though, when my own daughter was taken during a looting raid. I don't even know which group took her. She was beautiful, just on the edge of womanhood… I have not seen her in months." His eyes hardened.

"I'm sorry to hear that, *Señor* Del Rio," Storm said gently. His eyes and ears had been straining, trying to find a "tell," an indication of some lie within the story. So far, there was none. "Please, do go on."

"My men and I had gotten close to locating the Villalobos' hideout," Del Rio continued. "We had been working with a former member of their group, who had told us they had been moving the location of their camp, something about their need for a flowing source of water, and that they were using generators powered by hydroelectricity, which indicated to us that their operations were much bigger than we originally thought. With this informant on our side, we had never been closer to smashing them, and we began making plans to set off to the area our informant had indicated."

He chuckled bitterly. "That's when the previous police chief was murdered, and Panza appeared and took his position. He took over the investigation personally then, claiming that my men and I were mishandling it. We were taken off the case, and all files pertaining to the investigation were locked away. Shortly afterward, our informant was murdered, too."

"This whole thing stinks," exclaimed Skids. "It seems like you can't turn around in this country without getting stabbed in the back."

"Didn't you try to carry on the search yourself?" Willy asked Del Rio.

The detective shook his head. "Panza has watchers everywhere. I took a huge chance just by coming here today."

"And exactly why did you come here, *Señor* Del Rio?" Storm queried.

"Because I knew that if you were here looking for the Villalobos Brothers on behalf of Mr. Tolliver and Mr. Stein that you would come back here. I was worried, however, that you had been killed."

"Those fake cops we were with tried to do just that." Storm said. "They failed."

"What do you mean, Cliff?" Willy asked. "What happened out there?"

"We were set up. The 'hideout' we were checking out turned out to be a pre-dug mass grave dug just for us. Our police escort was all set to cut us down once we got there. We took care of them instead, but we're probably labeled as cop-killers by now."

"I was afraid of that," Del Rio said. "You now have effectively doubled your enemies here. I'd bet my entire career on this: Panza is not to be trusted. I've looked through files, made calls all over the island ever since he appeared... although there are some who vouch for him, there is no record of any Panza in any police files. Although he has supposed credentials, it is as though the man didn't exist before he turned up here in Templo Del Sol. I wanted to let you know at the police station, but I couldn't get to you in time before he led you away."

Stein stepped forward. "Now look here, Detective! Panza has assured me that he and his men have taken every step possible in their investigation. If you're thinking of accusing the chief of police of any kind of foul play..."

Storm held up his hand, cutting off Stein's protest. "Mr. Del Rio may be right here, Richard. The events that he- and now we- have encountered lead me to believe Panza may have some hand in things. We now know he can't be trusted, but I believe our friend here can be."

The detective's face was grimly set as he nodded. "Templo Del Sol is no longer a safe place for you, *Señor*. But then, you already know this." Del Rio pulled a sheet of paper from beneath his jacket and handed it to Storm. "These," he continued, "are the rough coordinates where our search for their hideout was to begin. It is very far from civilization, and you will need supplies for your excursion." He jotted a few lines on the paper. "I suggest you move quickly. When the hit squad you were with fails to check in with Panza, he will surely send more men. This house will be the first place he checks." He pointed at the sheet. "This is the frequency from my own personal radio set-up in my home. Please stay in touch and keep me informed."

Storm locked steady eyes with the detective's. "If the things you say are indeed the truth, *Señor* Del Rio, then you are taking a huge risk for us."

"I have to," he replied, shrugging. "I cannot search for this nest of vipers myself, as I am too closely watched, but your reputation precedes you. I know that you can do this." Anando Del Rio returned Storm's gaze and smiled warmly. There was a pause as the two men sized each other up as comrades who worked for the greater good, then Storm turned toward his team.

"Alright, we're getting out of here, troops," he said, then turned to the other two men. "Stein, Tolliver- you'll be coming with us, of course."

Tolliver moved to join Storm's men, but Richard Stein began his protesting anew. "So you're just going to pack up and leave on a wild goose-chase? You're going to trust him over the chief of police?"

Storm turned to the test pilot. "Yes, we are. We went to the chief of police here and almost got murdered... I'd say that's a great reason to trust him over Panza. Now pack your things quickly." His voice was commanding and cut off all further argument.

Stein went off into the rest of his bungalow to gather some belongings while Storm turned to Del Rio. "Detective..."

Del Rio was smoothing out his crushed hat and suit. "Later I will be going back to the police station to watch and wait from there." He smiled at the scarred countenance of the adventurer. "I wish I could join you, but I must remain here. I may be of help here; to... how do you say it, run an interference play?" He laid a hand on Storm's shoulder. "I know that this case is in the capable hands of a true ally now. Now go, and I will make sure you are able to leave the city as best as I can." And with that, he smiled devilishly and left.

The team did not gather their belongings from the hotel, as they were certain it might be under surveillance by now. Storm and his men were worried that their plane had been seized, but it was still there. The *Seeing Red* tri-motor had been serviced and refueled immediately upon their arrival on the island, so very little preparation would be required to get her in the air.

However, as they got closer to the dark airfield, their hopes for a clean getaway were dashed. Storm stopped their hired car at an inconspicuous distance as soon as he saw the pair of Templo Del Sol patrol cars parked just outside the fence. The group's car idled there, unsure.

"Cripes," Skids whined. "What do we do now?"

As if in answer, a light blinked toward them from a parked car. Alerted by the signal, the six men watched as a thin and furtive figure exited the signaling car and snuck over to the parked police autos. Their uniformed occupants stood a distance away, smoking cigarettes and talking and therefore unaware of the sneaking shape.

After a few moments, the wiry figure scrambled back to its waiting vehicle. The car started up and it tore away from the lot at high speed as the lounging policemen looked at its diminishing taillights curiously.

"Who the hell was...?"

Twin fireballs erupted from the empty patrol cars, cutting off Brock's query. The explosions tossed the automobiles in the air and knocked the policemen down, dazzling them with light and heat and stunning them.

Storm grinned. "Del Rio," he said.

He gunned the car's engine and the machine shot forward toward the field, rapidly passing the flaming diversions and the stunned cops. He crashed the car straight through the airstrip's gate and drove madly out onto the field, screeching to a halt beside the *Seeing Red* in a cloud of dust.

The men piled from the car and began hastily climbing into the plane. Beyond the fence, Storm could see the cops recovering. They stood and began to draw their pistols.

"Start her up, Skids!" he yelled after the blonde pilot, who scrambled into the pilot's seat and began racing through the checklist and start-up procedure. The new electric starters would shave time off their race for the air, but not much...

The cops were now running out onto the field now. There was no way to tell whether they were under the Villalobos Brothers' influence or just good and honest policemen doing their jobs, but Storm knew he had to slow them down as the engines were only now just starting up.

From his utility harness, Storm drew a small, tube-like flare-gun. Aiming it carefully to a spot in the sand just in front of the running pursuers, he pulled the trigger. The flare-gun emitted a whoosh of light and sound, and the red magnesium flare rocketed into the dirt before them and once again dazzled their eyes into temporary blindness. They fired their pistols wildly toward the plane.

At that moment, the *Seeing Red's* engines roared to life. The cops stumbled, still firing blindly, as the plane began rolling. Storm ran alongside it and leaped through the door, and Brock slammed it closed as soon as he was through.

In a few moments, the big plane heaved skyward, banking into the black sky. It was soon lost in the night.

"...the explosions...dazzling them with light and heat..."

INTERMISSION TWO

The train passenger shifted in his seat, muscles cramping a little from sitting for so long during the lengthening train ride. Setting the files on Storm aside for a moment, he got up and stretched and went to the washroom to splash some cold water on his face. Refreshed, he returned to his compartment to watch the scenery passing by the window for a few moments, hands in his pockets and deep in thought.

The *Zephyr* had outrun the grey weather and was now speeding along under sunshine and blue skies. The landscape was all rolling hills during this part of the journey, and the passenger reflected upon the life of Clifton Storm up to the point in the narrative he had developed in his mind while reading the chronologically-arranged files. Storm was a public figure by now, recognizable through his heroic deeds, but his past was largely unknown to most of the masses. There had been a lot of public conjecture, but this… this was the real story the passenger was learning now through his talent. The man behind the mystery was slowly being revealed to him as he read, as his mind plunged into its long trance and visions. The passenger begun to feel a little like a voyeur by this point, but that was normal for him. It was this synthesizing of facts that had made him such a valuable member of his organization, and no one was sure if it was simple intuition or something more. It had not gone unnoticed by the passenger's employers that he had come from a family history of psychic phenomena.

The passenger returned to his seat and picked up the next bit of information from the dossier: a document from the U.S. meteorological Bureau that detailed an unprecedented weather event that had blown into country during Storm's trip back home to Michigan…

A freak storm had ripped into the eastern United States, and with it came heavy snow and winds. The passenger plane that had departed from the defiantly sunny Florida climate found itself confronted by the icy front halfway over Georgia, and the chilly storm had been with the flight ever since. Attempts had been made to re-route the flight to avoid the weather, but it persisted and followed the plane like the shadow of destiny.

The aircraft, a Fokker F.VII, was full of talking and laughing passengers who chatted and joked about the pursuing storm. They were a diverse lot. The mix included newlyweds, vacationing couples, and two pairs of tired parents and their children (one of which was a newborn). A pair of elderly couples and an aging priest rounded out the passengers... except for one more.

Clifton Storm sat by a window and was oblivious to the friendly chatter around him. He stared through the glass and at the Smoky Mountain range below, blanketed by the swirling snow and thickening clouds.

The bleak weather mirrored his mind: since the telegram notifying him of his parents' deaths, his mind had been in a haze. He had packed and made return arrangements robotically, barely seeing or hearing those around him. Nothing felt real, as though he were living in some kind of dream.

His parents had been killed, and it had happened while he had been away and throwing himself into what probably would have been his last truly hedonistic and carefree outing before committing himself to the perceived shackles of college and responsibility. Before, he had resented his mother and father for threatening to cut off his wealth, but now they were gone. The family fortune was going to be left to him, and he knew this... but he never wanted this to happen. Not like this.

Beneath the haze of his mind, there were tiny stirrings of a new emotion, one truly foreign to Clifton Storm: guilt. It twisted and wormed its way through his selfishness, a pest, an itch he couldn't scratch.

The pilots of the plane had been experts, and they had tried their best to avoid the weather. No matter how high or low they went to avoid the icy clouds, they seemed to follow the plane, a dogged, hungry ghost. Through the windows, they had been able to see the glistening frost starting to appear on the leading edge of the Fokker's wings. It shone sporadically in the rising moon, a razor's edge...

Storm had been pondering his future as well as he could. What would he do now? After the reading of the will and the paperwork he would be left all alone with his parents' sprawling mansion. The servants would still be there... but he would still be alone... alone in the house, alone in the world. In more recent years he'd begun to drift away from his friends:

sometimes it was their doing, but mostly it was his due to his, falling into his own self-centered isolation. As much as he resented them and loathed their recent firmness, he had been closest to his parents. Beyond them he had no relationships, really. There were holes in his life that he was just starting to feel now.

Would he go on to college, now that this had occurred? He wasn't sure now. He couldn't envision himself going through the schooling, and yet what was the alternative? While he pondered this, a vision of an old, lonely miser drifted into his mind. Clifton Storm: decrepit multi-millionaire, a man with no use for a world that really had no use for him...

The droning of the Fokker's engines changed, deepening to a throb, and one element of the sound stopped. Storm looked forward out the window. Through the fog, he saw the port engine's propeller. It was stationary: it sat still and did not spin. Ice was caked around its base and the radial engine.

The mood aboard the plane changed drastically: the passengers began to question the flight attendant, who assured them everything was alright. When a passenger pointed out that one of the engines had ceased running, she had assured the group that the pilots could continue flying successfully with just two engines.

Several minutes later, the engine at the nose stopped as well, frozen by the chilly weather. The remaining engine on the starboard wing was not powerful enough to keep the craft aloft, and the Fokker began losing altitude.

In the cockpit, the pilots had struggled to keep the aircraft in the sky, but it was no use; slowly, the mountainous landscape was rising toward them. The crew hoped now for the only thing that could save them: to glide the craft down to a snowdrift or field, any place they could try to safely crash-land. The mountains, however, did not offer any such open area, and the snow-covered crags began to rise to meet the craft.

As the plane lowered from the heavens, the passengers became more chaotic and desperate. Pleading and crying mixed with murmuring and prayers, then intensified as the cruel winds among the peaks took hold of the shuddering plane. It shimmied as its wide wings were buffeted by the blasts of chilly air and the speed of its drop accelerated.

Still numb, almost glassy-eyed, Clifton Storm watched the events unfold, riveted to his seat in what seemed to be another phase of his long, dark nightmare...

Past the peaks the plane fell, panic reigning inside. The snow filled the pilots' windshield as they fought to keep the craft level. From out of the white haze, an outcropping of rock suddenly appeared. It sheared the starboard wing off in a shriek of rending metal. The jolting blow sent the airplane into a wild spin, and it whirled crazily through the air toward a rock formation.

The passengers were jerked about violently as loose items flew around the cabin, and a unified scream filled it. The last thing Storm saw through his window was a mass of stone heading for the side of the plane. There was a massive sledgehammer blow to the craft, the squeal of metal and splintering of glass, and a sudden pain and a heat that wasn't heat… then nothing. Blackness had closed around Storm.

CHAPTER 12:
HALTED, ONLY BRIEFLY

It would have been useless to begin the search for the Villalobos Brothers' hideout during the night, especially with a thunderstorm moving into the area. Instead, following the flight from Templo Del Sol, the crew of the *Seeing Red* searched for a place to camp overnight, far away from the city. They had swept the ground with a powerful searchlight mounted near the plane's cabin until they found a suitable clearing, which Skids was able to land the plane in with a minimum of bump and turbulence.

The storm blew in shortly after they landed, and they slept inside the plane that night rather than pitch their tents outside. It was cramped quarters due to the equipment and supplies that were packed within, and the thunder and lightning lasted throughout the night. The rain that pelted the aluminum aircraft was deafening, but eventually exhaustion overcame the men and they slept while the thunder and lightning boomed around them like a cannonade.

Morning found the group studying the maps of the island along with the coordinates that Detective Del Rio had given them.

Brock rubbed his chin thoughtfully and pointed to the area indicated by the coordinates. "Del Rio said that they needed running water, that his informant said they were moving toward a river or something... this spot doesn't indicate anything like that."

"I noticed that," Storm agreed. He compared the information once again, and the discrepancy between the coordinates and the aerial map still showed. La Isla de Sangre was still wild, a country that hadn't embraced a lot of the modern world too well, and thus the maps of the island were sometimes incomplete. What was in the spot on the map seemed to be just another unbroken stretch of jungle, and this was at odds with what Del Rio's informant had told him.

"So what do we do next?" asked Skids.

"We keep looking. It's worth a shot to snoop around where Del Rio is pointing us." Willy puffed on his cigarette and looked at Storm, who grinned back. The older man had spoken Storm's thoughts as he'd thought them himself. In need of counsel, he would often turn to Willy for advice. He respected his experience and opinions and this time, as on other occasions like it, the two men were on the same mental track.

"There's no river there," Stein protested. "I still think we're chasing our tails…" The handsome test pilot had been complaining the entire time they had been together, insisting that they attempt again to work with the police, to not only ferret out the crooked cops there but also to gain assistance in looking for the warlords.

"Mr. Stein," Storm interrupted. Their eyes met. "It's no secret that you disagree with our course of action here. This is our only lead at this point, though, and we're going to keep following it. Hopefully it will lead us to the Villalobos Brothers and Kate. If it doesn't, then we can start over again and you can tell us 'I told you so.' But until then, and with all due respect, please hold back your complaints. Keep them to yourself and let us do what we do best."

Silence hung in the air between them. Skids looked on with wide eyes, while Brock crossed his arms and Willy continued smoking. Storm and Stein stared at each other, the tension palpable.

Finally, Tolliver put his hand on Stein's shoulder.

"Richard… he's right. Let them handle this. They know what they're doing." The older man's voice was gentle, but Stein's jaw remained clenched.

"They'd damned well better," he said icily, then flinging Tolliver's hand off his shoulder he turned and stalked away.

Skids exhaled loudly. "Geez, what's his beef?"

Tolliver smiled and shrugged. "Richard can be hot-tempered and opinionated sometimes. He means well, really. I think he's just worried about Kate. Don't hold his actions over his head."

Shortly after their examination of the maps, the group packed up their temporary camp and piled into the *Seeing Red*. They were prepared to continue on to the search area. Storm started the engines, but as they were warming up there was an unusual shimmy to the plane.

"What's going on?" Willy asked, climbing into the cockpit.

"Feel that?" Storm asked of the shaking. "Starboard engine's got a problem."

"A big problem," Willy nodded, looking out the right side windows. "She's not turning over so good. Rotation's sluggish. What the hell...?"

Storm powered down the engines and the six men climbed from the plane. Upon inspecting the engine they discovered the problem.

"A stray bullet must have caught it," Willy said, peering at the neat hole punched into the engine housing. Upon removing the perforated panel, the extent of the damage was revealed: several lengths of piping had been ripped open, and oil and fuel drooled copiously into the guts of the engine. Skids cursed.

"How long, Willy?" Storm asked. His knowledge of mechanics was broad but nowhere near as intuitive as the older man's, although he was constantly striving to learn more.

"It's still early," he said, checking his watch and glancing at the sun. "If I get right on it, and with a little help, we can have her up in the air again by late afternoon."

Storm nodded. "Go ahead, then. You'll get your help, but not right away." He turned to the others. "Skids, you'll be scouting ahead in the *Witch*." He moved to the cargo hold with Brock; Skids followed but was stopped briefly by Tolliver.

"Skids... what's the *Witch*?" he asked, bewildered.

The short pilot grinned and chewed his ever-present wad of bubble-gum. "You'll see, Mr. T. She's black magic." He thumped Tolliver on the shoulder and winked at Stein, then moved off to join Storm and Brock as they began to unload equipment boxes from the *Seeing Red*.

The *Witch*, as it turned out, was one of the most unique aircraft that Tolliver and Stein had ever seen. It had been designed modularly, so that it could be packed up in several large crates for transport and for on-site assembly later. The assembly of the tiny plane took a little less than half an hour with Storm, Brock, and Skids building it.

Tolliver and Stein marveled at the small craft when it was finished: the *Witch* was a sleek single-person mono-winged design. Twin engines, small but powerful, reposed beneath the wings, and the whole plane was painted black with dark-red accents. At the nose were the little plane's name and her painted namesake: a shapely woman in a very brief witch's outfit riding a broom, complete with a pointed hat. A bright, girl-next-door smile was framed by her flaming orange hair.

"This is amazing," a stunned Tolliver said, staring at the diminutive aircraft.

"Good stuff, huh?" said Skids proudly as he put on a leather flying helmet. It was Storm who had designed the *Witch* and Willy and the MARDL engineers who had built her, but Skids was fond of the compact ship the most. As an air-racer, he was used to flying small and fast aircraft, and there were many times he wished he could fly the *Witch* in competitions.

"This tinker-toy plane actually flies?" Stein asked incredulously.

"You bet she does," answered Brock, wiping sweat from his brow.

"And she does more than just fly," Skids said to Stein with a grin. He didn't elaborate, however. He climbed into the cockpit and closed the canopy. The other men stepped back.

The small twin-engines roared to life and the little black-and-red airplane taxied off. In a few moments it gained momentum and lifted from the field and into the air. The landing-gear retracted, and the *Witch* made an incredibly tight turn before rocketing over their heads in the direction of the map coordinates.

Brock grinned at the plane dwindling in the distance. "Show-off," he said of his friend proudly.

The sun had climbed higher in the sky, reached its apex, and then had begun its descent. It was nearing 4:00.

As Willy had predicted, the repairs were winding down. The stray bullet had hit in a bad spot, the engine's wound doing as much damage as a single shot could. The repairs had been completed smoothly and quickly, however, and the *Seeing Red* could now fly again.

The men were just fitting the perforated engine-housing panel back into place when the radio crackled to life. It had been turned on when Skids departed. It had been silent since he left, but now it burst with sound and the Brooklyn-inflected voice of Skids Gerard came through.

"MARDL-two to MARDL-one… Cliff, are you there? Over."

Storm hurried to the wireless set and keyed the microphone. "It's Cliff, Skids. What do you have for us? Over."

The little pilot's infectious grin seemed to come through over the airwaves.

"For you, Boss, I got a canopy of trees. Below that: a valley. And in the bottom of that…" he paused to pop his gum, "…a beautiful, winding blue river. Over."

CHAPTER 13: REVOLUTION

Katherine Tolliver had been dozing. A thunderstorm had raged sometime during the night and had pummeled her tiny aluminum cell with rain, keeping her awake. At first, she had found sleeping to be hard in her captivity. The uncomfortable conditions kept her from doing anything but crouch or lay upon the dirt floor. Eventually, however, exhaustion made sleep possible, even in the oven-like confines of the cell.

After the storm, just after she had fallen asleep she had been woken by the sound of raised voices and the rumble of large trucks. From the snatches of conversation she had been able to make out, a large looting-party had returned from a conquest. She had also heard boasts and cheers. Apparently, they had succeeded in wiping out a rival group, the Pantera clan. This was both good and bad news. It was good because now there was one less group of guerrillas operating on La Isla de Sangre, but bad because the Villalobos Brothers were gaining power. They were dangerous to begin with, and now they were becoming more so. Something had shifted the power in the Villalobos Brothers' favor, and she had wondered what it could be... and if it could be stopped.

She had also heard, among the din, a woman's voice. She couldn't place the words, but by her tone she could tell she was being quietly resistant.

Eventually, the night's celebrations had died down. All grew quiet and Kate managed to sleep again.

She awoke to the now routine sounds of feet outside her door. She knew the sequence by now: the footsteps, the scrape of the lock, the door would swing open and the youngish-looking soldier would come in with her food. Maybe he'd take a bite of the food, or maybe he would throw it at her, but he always leered at her. The looks she got from some of the soldiers chilled her spine, although she had not been manhandled... yet.

She got into her most defensive crouch as she usually did. However, the face revealed to her when the door opened was that of a teenage girl, face bruised and eyes hopeless. She entered the cell with Katherine's food on its usual tin-plate. She avoided eye contact with the captive, but as she stooped to pick up the previous day's plate and chamber pot Kate grabbed her arm.

"Who are you?" Katherine asked of the startled girl in Spanish.

"Rosa," was her single reply.

"How did you get here?" she pressed further as the girl squirmed.

"I was taken by the Pantera clan. I was theirs until last night. Then, there were lights in the sky..." She stopped and shuddered.

"What? What happened?"

Rosa straightened and shook off Kate's grip. "They are gone now," she said simply. "I belong to the Villalobos Brothers now." She turned to leave.

"Rosa," Kate hissed in a whisper, lest the guards hear. The beaten girl turned. "I'm a friend. I'm not with them," she said, shaking her shackles for emphasis. "If you need to talk to anyone, I'm here." Katherine smiled at the newcomer, trying to reach out to the oppressed, even here. The girl turned away again and left, locking the door behind her, without another word.

Katherine dozed again for some time, until she was awakened by sound once again. This time, however, it was not the sound of her door being opened. Instead, it was the squelch and whine of feedback. A public-address system was being turned on, and she also heard dozens of gathered voices. "Everyone in the compound must be grouped outside," she thought. Laying her head on the dirt floor near the bottom of the pole she was chained to, she could just barely see under the door to her cell. A mass of booted feet were milling about outside, illuminated by the late afternoon sun.

Suddenly, the conversations ceased and cheers went up from the assembled crowd. A few moments later, an amplified voice boomed out from the speakers.

"*Hola*, friends," said the grating, amplified voice of Jorge Villalobos. It was met with shouted greetings that quickly died down. "As you know, last night we defeated the Pantera clan, our enemies to the south. From their bodies and from their ruins, we now have an expanded arsenal.

Our wallets grow fatter from their spoils, and we even have some more company now."

Harsh laughs came from the crowd. Queasily, Kate remembered Rosa's bruised face and dull eyes.

"Tonight," came another voice from the speakers. Esteban was speaking now: "Tonight we take on El Cráneos Del Infierno in the east. They are armed well, but should not be a problem for us now."

Another cheer from the rebels again. Kate squirmed. How could this be? The three groups had been warring for years now, battling in what was essentially a three-sided standoff. What could the Villalobos Brothers be using to shift that balance so fast? And what could her father possibly have had to do with it?

She recalled suddenly what she had learned from the locals and the rural families, the tales of slave-labor at the hands of the Villalobos Brothers' group, the confrontation with her father...

"Oh, Dad. No..." she breathed, as nausea crept into her belly.

"After tonight," Esteban continued, "no one will stop us. Who will stand in our way? Who *can* stand in our way? The police?" He grunted a laugh. "I have already seen to that. They will not make a move without my say so. A paltry royal guard is all the military our country has, and even they cannot stand in our way when we knock on their doors."

Kate's eyes widened. What were they saying? Could they be setting their sights beyond their simple territorial struggles?

The brutish Jorge Villalobos had the microphone again now, his tone rising in triumph. "No police... no military... not even the American interlopers, Challenger Storm and his team... NO ONE can stop us!" he shouted. Kate gasped at the mention of Storm. He was there? Going up against the warlords of La Isla de Sangre?

"We will march upon Templo Del Sol," Jorge continued. "We will march upon Calles Del Oro! We will march upon any village or town or hovel that dares to rise up against us!"

The crowd of fighters was whipped up into a frenzied state by this point, but what was said next sent them completely over the top.

"And when we march upon King Valencia's home," Esteban ranted, "he will have no choice but to give us the rest of his rule... the entire country of La Isla de Sangre... because he will have seen the might of the Villalobos Brothers... and the awesome power we wield, the power of *La Diosa de la Muerte!*"

Fierce war cries seemed to erupt from every throat as pistols and rifles shot into the air. The Villalobos Brothers' group was ready now, ready for war, ready to die for their cause of total domination. *This is no longer just territorial*, Kate thought. *What they're talking about now is a violent, bloody revolution!* Fear quaked within her for everyone on the island, and she continued listening for more clues, for information that could help her… if she ever got out of this mess alive.

CHAPTER 14: DISCOVERIES

The *Seeing Red* and the *Witch* skimmed over the treetops. Below, the lush jungle canopy stretched forth toward the mountains like an emerald carpet.

Skids had returned to the camp for refueling before the entire crew headed off again; this time he and the little plane would lead while the rest followed in the tri-motor. The pilot from Brooklyn, New York, whistled appreciatively as a flock of multi-colored birds, frightened by the planes, burst from the trees below like a puff of confetti.

"See?" Skids called over his microphone. "I told you guys it was a hell of a sight."

"It is pretty here," agreed Storm at the controls of the modified Ford. "But where is this river you told us about?"

"Just ahead, oh impatient one," Skids radioed back. "Just follow me. We're almost there." Ahead, a pair of mountainous peaks rose from the jungle. Between them was a huge gap in the foliage.

"Mind the dip," Skids said to the others, and angling the *Witch* into a slight dive he flew into the hole. Storm eased forward on the controls and the *Seeing Red* followed. Once through the gap, the jungle seemed to close above them. Below them, however, a hidden valley spread beneath their aircraft. Sunlight struggled through the leafy growth above, dappling the rocks and river that wound beneath the planes.

"No wonder no one's mapped this place from the air." Brock was staring though the windshield in rapt attention. "The jungle that's roofing it in is too thick."

"Skids said he saw some paths below," said Storm. "*Someone* knows this place is here."

"And they're not telling anyone, either," said Willy. "This would make somebody a perfect hideout." Tolliver and Stein said nothing; they sat and watched in awe and silence.

The two aircraft followed the river upstream. Skids had already followed it in the other direction and discovered nothing, save for where it emptied out into the sea. If there was a Villalobos base along the river's banks, it would have to be upstream.

They found several tributaries and smaller branching streams, but these turned out to be dead-ends. They continued concentrating their search on the main river as it wound through the valley like a glittering snake. Suddenly, the roof of vegetation above them stopped and unhindered sunlight streamed down. Beneath them the river widened here and seemed to be stronger.

Ahead, around the next bend in the valley, was an odd fog.

Storm was quiet, the impression of the coiled energy intensifying around him. "Everybody strap in," he finally said. "We don't know what's beyond that fog." Then, on the microphone: "Skids, you'd better get her ready. I'm too paranoid to not worry about ambushes and the like." "Gotcha, Boss," crackled the radio in response.

As he buckled the safety harness, Tolliver looked out the side window. Several rounded shapes on the *Witch's* fuselage were now popping open. These were evidently weapons pods, for the snouts of machine guns suddenly poked forth from the little plane's hull.

Storm and Skids throttled down their crafts, slowing them to a seeming near-crawl as they rounded the bend in the valley. The thick fog swallowed them up. Visibility was poor in the grey mist, and the droning of the engines was echoing eerily through the valley. Out the windows, the group was starting to notice the change in the valley walls. They had been grey stones and dirt, shot through with veins of La Isla de Sangre's ever-present scarlet clay. As they progressed further into this portion of the valley, the makeup of the walls were being replaced by an odd, reflective black stone. It gleamed back at them darkly through the mist like obsidian. Meanwhile, the mist intensified and thickened, and the men tried vainly to pierce the grey veil with their eyes and see beyond it.

"Wonder what those black clouds are from?" came the voice of Skids after long minutes in the fog. Ahead, there were indeed some black, nebulous shapes floating within the fog. They seemed to vary from the size of baseballs to massive house-sized forms. They drifted within the fog lazily as the planes began to fly among them.

Suddenly, something small and hard struck the leading edge of the *Seeing Red's* wing. "Those aren't clouds," Storm said.

"Aw, geez," Skids muttered.

Storm keyed the microphone. "Up," he said, a single terse word of command. Pulling back on the controls and pushing forward the throttle, Storm angled the tri-motor in a near-vertical climb. Skids did the same in his plane. The aircraft climbed together as the passengers of the Ford held tightly to their seats and safety belts. Still angled by the climb, Storm rolled the big plane to avoid a pair of dark shapes that threatened the wings. Skids followed the valley wall upward, toward the grey disk of the late afternoon sun shining through the fog.

Seconds ticked by tensely. "What's going...? Oh." Willy's query was cut short as one of the smaller "clouds" passed by the window rapidly... reflecting back the red and silver finish of the tri-motor.

Suddenly, the two airplanes broke out of the fog and leveled above the valley and the passengers could now see clearly, unhindered by the strange mist. Around and below them was a stunning scene: the valley was filled with floating boulders of various size and shape, all composed of the strange black stone that was the main component of the walls in the foggy section of the valley. The men looked on in awe as the rocks floated gently in the wind. A pair of automobile-sized boulders collided gently, sending each other back in opposite directions.

Willy pointed out the port side of the tri-motor's windscreen. "Whatever's making those rocks float, it isn't permanent. Look."

Their gaze followed his and they saw a medium-sized rock as it dropped from its floating position and began to plummet downward. It bounced off the valley wall and continued down into the fog to the river below.

"What the hell is that stuff?" Storm breathed. He turned to his passengers. Tolliver looked sick, his grey hair matted down with sweat. Richard Stein returned Storm's gaze blankly.

Returning his eyes to the valley, Storm noted the sun's low position. "Skids, let's find a place to land. We don't want to be flying around in the dark with these rocks buzzing around in the sky with us."

Night had fallen. Clifton Storm and the others sat around a campfire eating their dinner. The spot where they landed for the night was right at the edge of the valley. In the distance they could hear vague rumblings and cracking sounds as the floating rocks bumped into each other or fell into the valley below. In the dark they could also now see that the floating

"What the hell is that stuff?"

rocks emitted a faint purple glow, this glow; just before one of the rocks fell, this weird glow would fade out and the rock would grow dark. It was an eerie setting for their camp, and the group was quiet during their meal, unsettled by their surroundings.

When their dinner was finished, Richard Stein announced that he was tired and would be settling down for bed shortly. He made his way to the parked *Seeing Red* to gather some of his things. Brock, Willy and Skids began pitching the tents, leaving Storm and Tolliver together sitting on opposing sides of the camp-fire.

There were several minutes of silence, broken only by the calls of nighttime insects and animals and the distant sounds from the mystery rocks. The campfire crackled softly, and Tolliver was staring at it thoughtfully. He let out a heavy sigh and raised his eyes, and met Storm's gaze. Tolliver smiled nervously and looked away, and in that moment Storm made his decision.

"There's a bit more to all this than we've been led to believe, isn't there?" he asked the older man.

Tolliver opened and closed his mouth, attempting to maintain an air of innocence and perplexity. The scarred face and piercing eyes held him, however. He felt like a bug pinned down for examination; something in Storm's gaze seemed to strip away Tolliver's false pretenses and to lay bare the truth, no matter how he tried to hold it in. Finally, the tycoon dropped his gaze again. "How... how long have you known?"

"I've had a feeling since the very beginning, in my office," the adventurer replied. "You seemed reluctant to come for our help, and much more nervous than a powerful businessman like yourself should have been." Storm picked up a stick and absently poked it into the fire. "Willy saw it too," he said, "but the real clincher for me was today. You didn't seem to be very surprised by those rocks in the sky, only scared that we would collide with them." He looked back at Tolliver.

The tycoon could sense his gaze, but did not raise his eyes. "What do you want to know?" he asked.

Storm moved to a seat closer to Tolliver. "Everything...and start at the very beginning, if you please."

CHAPTER 15: REVELATIONS

Tolliver sighed again, the full weight of his story heavier now than ever.

"It started when my company, White Heron Aviation, was asked by the U.S. government to cease production on the Valkyrie bomber," he began. "That was to have been THE contract, the one that would have moved White Heron from just a commercial company and into the lucrative field of military contracting. The company was already making a lot of money, but the Valkyrie contract... that would have pushed our company's profits into the stratosphere. We... I... was severely troubled by the loss of the project."

Tolliver raised his eyes to the night sky. "Then, without any warning, the Army announced the planning of a new plane, the Paragon, with an open competition to all manufacturers to produce a prototype. Apparently, this model was to have taken the place of the Valkyrie, which the government viewed as already outdated. We worked on coming up with a set of plans... amazingly, from what my sources tell me, White Heron was actually the only company to have even come close to producing a working design... and that's where my troubles really began."

He picked up a small rock. It was a smooth black stone of the same material that was floating in the valley. He smiled grimly at the stone and flung it into the darkness; in the distance, it struck the ground with a soft plunk.

Storm waited patiently for him to continue his story. Behind them in the camp, Skids tripped over the guide-line of a tent, and Brock exploded into laughter, a mirthful sound that momentarily brightened the bizarre setting of the eerie valley.

Tolliver cleared his throat and continued: "Shortly after White Heron began working on the new plane's design, I came to Las Isla de Sangre to visit Kate. While I was here, I was approached by some men who somehow knew of the project... they had to be industrial spies, I figured. They offered to help me construct the prototype aircraft."

"The Villalobos Brothers?" Cliff smiled.

"Yes... how did you guess?" the tycoon asked.

"Just a hunch," he replied. "Please go on."

"Yes, well..." Tolliver continued, "The nature of this plane that the government wanted us to build requires it not just to hover, but to have complete directional freedom and mobility in any direction as well. It seemed that we weren't any closer to that goal, but the Villalobos Brothers offered me a way to make the Paragon be able to do just that."

"Wait," Storm stopped him. "Exactly what kind of airplane is this?"

Tolliver looked uneasy. "The Army described their idea as an aerial gunnery platform," he explained. "Instead of merely bombing a target, the plane was to be designed to fly to the target's location and simply bombard it with weapons fire from a stationary position in the air." As he spoke he demonstrated the idea with hand-gestures. "It was to carry bombs, yes, but also numerous large-caliber machine guns and even mounted howitzer cannons. And the fuselage itself would be heavily armored from return fire. Airships are impractical for this because of the dangerous gases, and a true-gyro hasn't been perfected yet, but this plane would have fit their needs. What they wanted was a complete, mobile, flying battle-station."

Storm nodded, deep in thought and picturing such a craft. "Go on."

"Well, the Brothers... their reputation is well-known here. My daughter and Richard, they knew of them as the prime terrors of the island, blood-thirsty and power-mad warlords. They would have kept me from talking to them, of course, so I simply didn't tell them of the meeting." He chuckled softly. "When all you see is dollar signs in your eyes, you don't want to see anything but that money. I was a fool."

Tolliver paused to rub his tired eyes. "I met them and they took me here, to this valley. It's a place that the locals shunned for so long that they've nearly forgotten it was here. They're superstitious of it. They think it's haunted, because of the ore." He indicated the floating rocks in the distance. "Because of the Skyrock."

"How does it work?" Storm asked quietly.

Tolliver picked up another small shard of the black stone. "If I simply pick up this piece of Skyrock and drop it…" he paused to let it fall from his right hand into his left, "…nothing. And I could throw it with as much force as possible and still it would eventually fall, just like any other gravity-obeying object. And yet," he held up the shard and turned to Storm. "If charged with electricity, the stone's unique properties cause it to levitate. And it will stay levitating, at whatever level you hold it at last, until the charge wears off."

"Then those stones and boulders out there," Storm gestured toward the valley, "Those were charged by last night's thunderstorm?"

"Correct. What you saw out there were pieces of Skyrock that had been struck by lightning during the storm, and some probably even just picked up the static electricity in the air for their charge."

"There were a lot of floating rocks out there," Storm said.

Tolliver nodded. "An unfortunate side-effect of the mineral: it actually attracts the lightning. Also," he continued, "the flow of electricity is important. If it's a quick charge, such as the lightning, the stone will float for a long while and eventually drop. If the flow is well regulated, it will levitate indefinitely. If the ore is charged and continues to be so without any regulation…" he tossed the piece of Skyrock in his hand. "It will go up and keep going up… into orbit. It's a delicate science, and a new field. This island is the only place in the world to find the stone, and modern life is slow to come here. Scientists have yet to get their hands on this stuff. That was to be my edge, an ace in the hole that was to be mine and no one else's."

Tolliver's eyes seemed distant now as he studied anew the piece of Skyrock in his hand. "What the Villalobos Brothers offered to me seemed like an answer to my prayers. They stated their price… it was hefty, even by American standards, but it would pale in comparison to what White Heron would be pulling down once we completed the Army's prototype. They assured me that what I would pay would go towards their expenses in the mining of the ore. I accepted and began to pay them, then started drawing up the plans for the new craft, one that would take advantage of the Skyrock's abilities."

Tolliver's eyes darkened. "At first," he went on, "everything seemed to be running smoothly. The Villalobos Brothers routinely called me in America to update me on how much Skyrock was being produced. It was slow going at first, and they couldn't give me a timetable for when the first shipment of processed Skyrock ore would be available for delivery to White Heron. I sat on my secret, telling nobody else of the amazing find that would make us rich. And while I sat and waited, I paid them patiently."

The night became still, as if it too were listening to the unfolding tale. "I had scheduled a trip to the island, but a call from my daughter brought me back to it much sooner than I expected. As I've already told you, Kate was very much loved by the people here for her educational work. They would often confide in her things they couldn't or wouldn't tell the local police, for fear of those on the Villalobos Brother's payroll." Tolliver smiled. "They should make my Katherine a saint.

"The people she worked with began telling Kate about disappearances and kidnappings, about rumors that were coming from the less civilized areas of the island... rumors that the Villalobos Brothers were collecting slaves for a large project." The tycoon suddenly found it hard to look at anything but the ground at his feet.

"Your Skyrock," Storm said.

Tolliver nodded without looking at him. "You're right. At first, I didn't want to believe it, and then..." he paused, "...then, I just didn't care. I didn't see it, it wasn't me or any of my family or friends... it wasn't even any of my own countrymen that it was happening to. I just knew that the Villalobos Brothers were producing the Skyrock ore that I could use to make the building of the plane a reality. White Heron would produce the plane, we'd get our contract, and we'd all be rich. I was a fool," he said sadly. "Kate kept looking into it, and it wore away at me. My guilty conscience finally became too much too bear and I broke down."

The tycoon took a deep breath. "I contacted the Villalobos Brothers and arranged a meeting with them. I demanded better conditions for their workers, or that they set them free and I'd bring in my own workers from the States. I threatened to pull my funding if it didn't happen. I was stern, I was staunch and unyielding. I thought they would give in to my demands... but I forgot I was dealing with criminals. They laughed at me."

When he next spoke, Tolliver's voice sounded small, as though a young child was speaking from within him.

"As I've already told you, Katherine was already a target because of her educational work. The Villalobos Brothers had clearly tried to scare her away from snooping around with their threats... they didn't work. They kidnapped her then, when I threatened to back out of the deal. They began holding her ransom to force me to continue my payments to them. If I stopped paying them or if I went to someone for help..." Tolliver's voice cracked with emotion as he trailed off. His eyes were filling with tears.

"I'm sorry, Mr. Storm. I'm sorry I didn't care when I heard about the slaves. I'm sorry I waited so long to stand up to the warlords. I'm sorry that I waited so long to tell you this, the truth. I'm so sorry."

The older man buried his face in his hands and wept from his guilt and shame. Storm watched him silently; he was all too familiar with the throes of regret, and the effects of those emotions had turned J. Gordon Tolliver from a powerful and confident business man into a shell of a person, wrecked from the inside out.

"Mr. Tolliver," Storm said at last. The tycoon raised his head. "It's never too late to apologize," the adventurer told him, "and never too late to make up for mistakes you've made. Don't doubt for a moment that my men and I will keep going. We'll still get Kate back for you, Mr. Tolliver. We'll stop the Villalobos Brothers."

"Thank you!" Tolliver gushed in gratitude, leaping to his feet and shaking Storm's hand vigorously. "But, what about the others, your crew…"

"I'll tell my men your story tonight," he assured the aviation magnate. He looked toward the tent that would house Tolliver and Stein, who was already bedded down for the night inside. "What about Kate's fiancé? Have you told him this tale yet?"

"No," Tolliver shook his head. "I am afraid he'll hate me for putting Katherine in danger. I will tell him, though. Tomorrow I'll fill him in."

Storm nodded and stood up. "Good. I can see that he can be difficult. If there are any problems, we can deal with him together."

With that, Tolliver thanked Storm again and left to prepare for bed. Storm, meanwhile, sat down with Brock, Willy, and Skids and told them the details of Tolliver's story that had been revealed to him. Although they admitted to feeling betrayed by their client, none of them could argue that in the end Tolliver had done the right thing. The fact that the Brothers had used such cowardly maneuvers had incensed them even more to stopping the island's guerrilla group. Their resolve was strengthened.

Several hours after the party had bedded down for the night, a curious scene unfolded in the darkened campsite.

Stealthily, the form of Clifton Storm left his tent. He paused outside the tent holding J. Gordon Tolliver and Richard Stein, and he listened to their deep, slumberous breathing for a while. When he was satisfied that they were truly sound asleep, he silently entered the *Seeing Red* tri-motor and closed the door.

Sometime later, he emerged from the plane as quietly as he entered it. In his hand was a small package, which he deposited in his pocket. He returned to Stein and Tolliver's tent again and listened. After once again determining that its occupants slumbered deeply, he cautiously and slowly entered the tent.

Long minutes passed. The occupants did not stir and kept on snoring, and so they were oblivious to Storm's presence.

Eventually, Storm exited the tent and crept to his own. Outside the tent, he exhaled with relief and wiped away sweat that had beaded on his forehead. He had been tense and careful during his stealthy actions; now he finally relaxed.

After gazing at the sky for several long moments in contemplation, Storm yawned and stretched, then entered his tent and promptly fell asleep after lying down.

CHAPTER 16: "THERE IS NO HOPE..."

atherine Tolliver awakened to the sound of shouts and cheers, instinctively crawling as far as she could away from the door of her cell. Outside, there was another celebratory commotion. From the din of voices and sounds, she was able to pick out one repeated phrase... *"¡Los Cráneos del Infierno han caído!"* "The Skulls of Hell have fallen!"

A wave of loss washed over her. It was official now: the Villalobos Brothers, once part of a three-way power struggle between La Isla de Sangre's warlords, now stood alone. They had been able, with whatever their "Goddess of Death" was, to vanquish their last group of rivals. Their next step was to take on the government and the people.

The revelry and celebration continued. Fighting off the fear and sadness at the triumph of her captors, she finally managed to doze back off and sleep for a while in a fitful and disturbed slumber. However, the scrape of the lock on her cell-door awoke her. It was the middle of the night, certainly not time to eat. She prayed it would be the new girl, Rosa, who opened the door.

It was not.

In the opened doorway stood the youthful guard who had delivered her food to her cell before Rosa arrived. He swayed there drunkenly, a nearly empty bottle of whiskey in his hand. He leered at Kate with his cruel eyes, and a churning feeling came to the pit of her stomach.

The soldier advanced, mumbling nearly incoherently. He dropped the bottle onto the dirt-floor and abruptly grabbed Kate by the hair, forcing her head back. She gasped from the sudden pain and he covered her mouth with his own before she could protest... but this lasted only a moment. The soldier screamed as Kate bit down on his tongue. He reeled back, blood gushing from between his teeth. With an oath, he lunged back at Kate, lust and hate and murder in his eyes...

Suddenly a blur of silver struck his head, stunning him. He fell to his knees and looked up. Esteban Villalobos held his silver-headed cane in a white-knuckled fist, anger burning in his face. He stooped to pick up the whiskey bottle and seemed to contemplate it for a moment then whirled suddenly and struck the soldier across the face. The bottle shattered, and the soldier screamed as bits of glass sliced into his face. He collapsed and lay flat, moaning in pain and frantic, drunken apologies.

Esteban called out to a pair of guards who stood outside the cell. They dragged the bloody soldier out. Kate grabbed a large shard of the broken bottle from the dirt and hid it while Esteban watched the guards, keeping it near in case she needed it. When they left, the dapper warlord closed the door behind them, and then turned to face Kate. There was silence as the two locked eyes.

"Your father will be here soon," he finally said.

Kate's face went blank. A million thoughts whirled in her head.

"He's being brought here tomorrow," Esteban continued, "along with your fiancé and the Americans who have been brought in to help. We are giving your father one last chance to keep you alive. When he sees you and how close you are to those... animals," he nodded toward the door, "he will have no choice but to keep paying us."

"Paying?" Her throat was dry, and the word came out in a croak.

"Oh, yes," he smiled, teeth showing pearly white in his sun-browned face. He picked a bit of dirt from his immaculate jacket and began then to talk.

He told her of the meetings with her father, about the Skyrock, the deal that was struck between him and the Villalobos Brothers. He told her of the slave-labor, of her father's lack of concern for them. He told the entire tale, everything that Tolliver had told Clifton Storm. He also told her more, though, things which Tolliver had been unaware of, secret pieces of the puzzle. He told her of coming plans.

The entire time, Katherine Tolliver felt her heart sinking, the last glimpses of hope dwindling. She felt rage, frustration, helplessness. Most of all, she felt betrayal, a hot and sickly-feeling in her stomach.

She started to cry, eyes cloudy with bitter tears. "Why did you tell me all of this?"

Stroking his mustache, Esteban replied: "So that you know that there is no hope for you. So that you can let your father know when you see him tomorrow that the only way you can live is through his continued support of our group." He bowed curtly and turned to the door. "Now rest," he said with a tone that was as silky as it was sarcastic. "Daddy's coming to see you tomorrow."

He departed, and Kate cried alone in her cell. Hope had fled, and the future looked bleak.

Outside, a drunken Jorge Villalobos began beating his pet wolves again, their yelps and screams echoing through the humid jungle night.

CHAPTER 17: MURDER IN THE JUNGLE

Morning had come.

The rescue party had been roused from sleep by the rising sun, and they all agreed that their sleep was strangely deep for the odd surroundings they had camped in. They took down their tents and prepared breakfast. During the morning activities, Clifton Storm was aloof and distant from the rest of the party. He spent a lot of time walking along the edge of the valley, looking down the embankment and into the misty river below.

Tolliver asked Skids about their leader's distance from the group. "Don't worry about Cliff, Mr. T.," he replied. "He gets quiet and moody like that sometimes. It usually means he's thinkin' something over."

When breakfast was finished, Tolliver looked to Storm, who nodded and smiled gently. Tolliver heaved a big sigh as Storm walked back to the edge of the valley, seemingly lost again in thought. Tolliver turned to Stein.

"Richard," his voice cracked. "I have to tell you something. This whole thing is… my fault. I made a deal with the Villalobos Brothers to help construction of the Paragon attack plane, the one I told you about. I…"

Stein held up a hand, stopping the tycoon. "Mr. Tolliver, save it. I already know this story." He smiled, and something was different behind his eyes.

Willy, Skids, and Brock stopped their packing activities. "You do?" Willy asked, and he was suddenly tense. Storm looked on from his spot by the ledge.

"Of course," the test pilot replied. His smile changed, his leading-man looks suddenly became devilish. He turned back to Tolliver.

"Who do you think put them onto you? Or told them about the

Paragon plane, or suggested Kate as leverage to be used against you? You incompetent old man…"

"Richard…," Tolliver stammered, unable to believe that his confidant, his future son-in-law, was the instigator, the behind-the-scenes manipulator that started the events they were now caught up in.

Sensing Storm's men approaching from the right, Stein whipped his pistol out from where it had been tucked into his waistband at his back. "Don't," he told them without turning, leveling the gun at Tolliver's chest. "Not unless you want to see this old fool develop a sudden heart problem." His darkened grin was frozen on his face like a mask of evil.

"You never stopped to wonder about it, did you?" Stein continued to Tolliver. "Of course not; all you could see was the money you'd be making off of the Paragon. Well, there is money coming in from that contract, but it damned sure isn't going to be yours."

"What do you mean?" Tolliver was pale, nearly unable to look away from the pistol that loomed large in front of him. His fear, however, was turning into a bright knot of rage.

"Your plans: I knew where you kept them, and I copied them… twice. With one set of the plans I plan to begin construction of my own variation of the Paragon to present to the army. I'm beating you to that contract, Mr. Tolliver, and you're going to let me beat you to it."

"And the other set of plans?" Storm asked. He stood stock-still, watching every move that Richard Stein made.

"All that slave-labor wasn't just for the mining of Skyrock," he replied. "The Villalobos Brothers see this island, all of La Isla de Sangre, as their birthright… and they've already begun to reclaim it. They're taking it back, using Mr. Tolliver's plane. They have their own version of the Paragon. They call it *La Diosa De La Muerte*… the *Goddess of Death*. They've already taken down their rivals… their next target is none other than the king and the entire capitol, Templo del Sol. Who knows? They may even expand their territory to all areas of South and Central America.

"Now we're all taking a walk. The Brothers' compound isn't too far away from here at all by foot. Start walking, Mr. Tolliver." He cocked the hammer on his automatic to show his prisoners that he wasn't playing around. "You'll lead the way."

"I knew you stunk from the moment I met you," Storm said. "I just knew that behind the pretty-boy mug and the legendary reputation beat the tiny, shriveled heart of a weasel." He took a step toward Richard Stein, who shifted his stance so that he was facing Storm past Tolliver.

"I'd advise you to tread carefully, Mr. Storm. I assure you I will ventilate Mr. Tolliver unless you behave yourself."

"No you won't," the adventurer said assuredly. "That's only the last resort. The one you really want to shoot here is me." He smiled.

"Boss..." Brock started.

"Can it, all of you," Storm told his men. "Richard Stein is a little yapping lap dog who would love nothing more than to take out the leader of the pack." He lowered his voice threateningly. "C'mon, little rich boy. We've been butting heads since we first met, and not just because you were trying to stop us. I'll give you your chance." He took another step.

Stein turned the gun toward Storm. The tension in the humid air magnified. "You know that I will shoot you dead." He said to his target evenly.

"Yes," Storm replied. "I know you want to, but I doubt you can." He tensed visibly to lunge.

Stein pulled the trigger three times, the booming pistol shots ringing through the air and echoing through the valley. Storm's lunge halted abruptly, and he twisted, spun, convulsed... and fell limply from the ledge, into the valley below.

The normally placid Brock shouted "No!" and attempted to leap at the gunman, his hands eager to rip out the test pilot's throat. Willy and Skids were just as devastated as their comrade was, but were able to hold him back as Stein spun and covered them with his weapon. It was an intense struggle for the two men to hold him, but they managed.

"Don't do it, Brock," Willy advised the giant strongman. "He'll kill us too... and we need to stay alive to finish this." He glowered at Stein.

Skids disdainful stare echoed Willy's. "He's right, Brock. We gotta stick around to make Mr. Hotshot there pay for what he did."

Stein laughed. "I seriously doubt you will." Still holding his aim on the troubleshooters, he stepped to the edge of the valley and peered down. Beyond the precipice where Storm had fallen was only a blank wall of dirt and blood-red clay, shot through with veins of the black Skyrock. Tiny rivulets of falling sand were the only thing that marked where the body of Clifton Storm must have rolled several moments before. Satisfied, Stein turned back to his captives.

"Okay, gentlemen," he told them. "This little show is over and I'm in charge here now. Hand me your guns and line up in a straight line, tallest to shortest, so I can watch all your backs. And I don't have to tell you…" he grinned, "no funny business."

The men lined up as they were told and began to march across the camp and toward the jungle. It was all they could do. The shooting of their leader had stunned them, and the only hope they had was to somehow get free and finish the mission to rescue Tolliver's daughter and stop the Villalobos Brothers. Extracting vengeance on Richard Stein was now on the list of their objectives as well.

When they reached the edge of the clearing, the line paused as Willy, Skids, and Brock turned to look one more time toward the spot where Storm had fallen. They knew there was no hope: he had been shot at point-blank range three times, and had been wearing no bulletproof vest. In their minds, his sickening and twisted fall replayed over and over again.

"Get going," Stein growled to the four captives.

Reluctantly, the men turned and stepped into the thick growth of trees and foliage. In a moment, they had been swallowed by the plants and were gone, disappearing into the green hell of La Isla de Sangre's jungle.

INTERMISSION THREE

Outside the windows of the speeding *Zephyr*, night had fallen. The passenger had turned the lamps on, bathing his private compartment in a warm glow of yellow light. He stared straight ahead at the opposite wall now. He was concentrating on removing himself from the trance he had placed himself in during the perusal of Storm's dossier… and was finding it difficult, his mind dwelling on the events that he had witnessed with his second-sight.

Nobody but Storm and the passengers knew exactly what happened on the Fokker's ill-fated flight across the Smoky Mountain range, and those other passengers couldn't tell their stories now. Perhaps it was conjecture on the part of the *Zephyr*'s passenger that drew the events before his mind's eye, perhaps it was the much-vaunted "intuition" that his employers valued in his case-study work such as this. Or, perhaps, it was the ability to see the events as they had actually occurred through some kind of psychic anomaly that he was blessed with. In either case, the passenger himself didn't know how he did it, and he really didn't care. All he knew was that it worked correctly 99 percent of the time and that it was good enough for his line of work.

The passenger blinked and stood, looking out the window again and this time seeing darkness, broken occasionally by the lights of distant houses and the stars above them. He was tiring out, as he often did during the examination of a subject's biography and its subsequent trance, but he wanted to finish the file as soon as possible. The events within the dossier seemed to be rushing ahead at breakneck speed, and he wanted to be done with them before he took his dinner and went to sleep for the night.

He sighed and sat down again, rubbing his eyes before settling them once again upon the files. He began reading, and the night outside the train seemed to give way to another night, years before, experienced by another…

Clifton Storm awoke to a feeling of piercing, screaming pain.

His body was sore, tender from countless bruises, and his skull ached as though it was being squeezed in a vise. The worst sensation, however, came from the left side of his face and neck: the fiery pain of sliced flesh and the cold and wet feeling of blood oozing down his neck…

He sat up slowly, as each movement brought a fresh symphony of agony to his nerves and his head swam with dizziness. With an effort he took in his surroundings and his mind struggled to find equilibrium. He was sitting in a clearing; snow was on the ground and falling all around him. He realized that the snow on his left side was soaked crimson with blood and he hesitantly brought his left hand up to touch his face. Bloody, ragged skin met his fingertips and brought a fresh stab of pain. He gingerly counted the wounds: three long and deep gouges, lined up as though an enormous cat had clawed the left side of his face. The first and third cuts ended at his jaw line, while the one in the middle ran from his temple like the others but extended past his jaw, down his neck, and stopped short just before reaching his collarbone. This cut had just narrowly missed Storm's carotid artery. If this cut had been just a fraction of an inch closer it would have killed him, spilling his lifeblood out into the snow around him.

He dimly became aware now of pieces of metal, debris and random objects. Pieces of the crashed plane surrounded him. He stood dazedly, shaking, and turned around.

A distance away, he saw the Fokker. The aircraft was barely recognizable. When its left side collided with the rocks it had split open, its crumpled aluminum fuselage spilling out debris… and people.

Storm's shaking legs gave way, and he knelt in the bloody snow. All around him was carnage and destruction, ragged metal and ragged flesh peppered with debris and soaked with blood and spilled fuel. A tree had somehow caught fire during the crash, and the firelight lent a ghoulish aura to the scene. He looked in vain for movement, for someone… anyone… who was left alive. He called out, his voice shaking and small in the emptiness. He called again, louder, and was returned nothing but an echo from the mountains. There was no one left; he was alone in the snow and silence with the dead.

He steeled himself and stood, stumbling now through the bodies and wreckage. He counted the corpses as he encountered them, hoping perhaps someone was unaccounted for, that someone was left besides him. They were all there, though, even the children.

Storm moved away from the carnage and sat down with his back against a rock. He drew his knees up to his chest as the frigid air whipped around him. His mind was blank, shocked. He wasn't sure how long he sat there... minutes, hours. Time had no meaning for him, and everything seemed distant and detached.

Eventually coherent thought gradually returned to his numbed brain and he found himself coming back to his senses...

He found that his eyes strayed again continually to the bodies. As if being visited by their ghosts, he pictured them alive, laughing and chatting about the weather and the little trivialities that had probably seemed so pointless and small and inconsequential to them while still alive... but were now so important, those fleeting moments like gold. Life was frail, and those little moments were now so much bigger, so precious to those who died. Each moment in life had been brief and essential and special... and now they were gone for those who died.

His mind drifted, eventually focusing again on his own predicament. And what of his own life, he wondered. A lifetime spent reveling in heady and selfish moments, so cold and empty now in comparison to the little, mundane, precious lives of the dead passengers and crew. He had watched the world outside of his own with disdain and detachment. Life... *real life...* had gone on around him and he'd cared for nothing in the world but his own happiness at all costs. And now he was truly alone, in his life and on this mountain, in this world. He was going to perish, unworthy of the time he had spent and had taken for granted. Unworthy of the life that he'd been given and squandered only on himself.

Or had he been left alive instead, still on Earth for a purpose? He had been spared, given another chance at life. Apart from the wounds that he knew would scar him for life he was untouched and uninjured, allowed to continue living. If he was smart and resourceful, perhaps he could survive; maybe he could make it out of the mountains and live the rest of his life. "But why was I spared?" he pondered. The people on the plane with him had had lives, families, children, careers. Those people with so much to live for had been snuffed out of existence, and yet he was allowed a second chance. Did he deserve it? *No*, he thought: *a life that had been lived so shallowly, so full of its own worth didn't deserve to continue...* at least, not on the path he had been on. But was there a way he could make his life count?

This was a crucial moment in his life, he realized, a moment that he could never back down from if he made his decision to alter the way he

"Time had no meaning for him..."

had been traveling. He couldn't simply make apologies or give to charities; he knew that those gestures just wouldn't be enough for him to justify his worth. For his life to count, to justify his continuing existence, he would have to be a true catalyst of change and betterment to other people in the world. He was still young, with a lot of time left on earth; he could be a virtual blank slate from here on in, a fresh start with a new direction. The funds at his disposal were vast and his proper schooling in the world was about to begin. His parents had tried to help the world as much as they could, and he could keep their memories and their saintly wishes alive by continuing their work. People still needed help in the world, and sometimes nobody would stand up for them. But now he could... and would. He would throw himself into the improvement of the world, the assistance of others, and the punishment of those who would prey upon the helpless and needy... people as cold and ruthless and empty as he had been. He pictured the possibility: a crusade that perhaps others of a like mind would join, a unified force for making differences in the world for everyone. And it would all start, here and now, with him.

He stood up, the shakiness and pain and weariness suddenly gone from his body, the cold and chill seemingly miles away. He was a new life, stark and clean and bright in the snowy night as he embraced his epiphany. Clifton Storm was reborn.

The lost flight was big news, and search parties had been organized when the weather cleared up enough to go in and look. The search planes crisscrossed the Smoky Mountains repeatedly until they finally located the wreckage. When the searchers on the ground reached the site, they found an odd scene. The bodies of the crash victims were found methodically buried, some with their identification secured to them. They were able to check the bodies against the passenger list; when the body of the only passenger not accounted for failed to turn up, it gave them a clue to who had buried the corpses so respectfully.

Clifton Storm, heir to one of the largest fortunes in America, was missing. It made the papers and tabloids as big news and captured the public's attention, so much so that when he wandered from the mountains two weeks after the crash, his story of survival was expected to generate even more sensational news.

And so it was a shock to the public when Storm declined interviews and shunned the spotlight, disappearing from the public eye.

Storm's survival and journey through the mountains had had a profound effect on his appearance. Unable to sew his wounds, his facial cuts had healed to become large marring scars, but there were other, more intangible signs of change. An almost palpable energy seemed to radiate from him now, as though he were vibrating with some inner-purpose. His eyes had changed as well: no longer flinty and cold, they were now steely with determination and warm with eagerness. Their newfound depth told anyone who looked into those eyes that they were older than they should have been and that they had seen much in a very short period of time.

Returning to the rest of the world Storm officially inherited his parent's fortune, after which he promptly made large donations to the victims of the crash.

College was next: he attended as originally scheduled, but he flourished in his schooling where his former self would have languished. His fields of study were varied, and he dove into each course with a hunger bordering on mania. Chemistry, engineering, anthropology, archaeology, law... all were devoured by his ever-questing mind. Extra-curricular activities- archery, fencing, wrestling, track and field- all were tackled with the same ferociousness, the same drive for self-improvement and betterment of himself and of the world. He shunned most companionship, keeping but a few close friends. He was the "big man on campus"... he was virtually famous but was seemingly invisible, rarely seen by classmates outside of his classes.

He ended his college years as everyone who knew of him thought he would: with the highest possible honors and accolades. His training was not done, however, and once again Storm disappeared from public view.

He was rarely seen during the next four years, but he did pop up from time to time: throughout Europe at first, then in exotic corners of the Orient. Rumors of a scar-faced man with intense blue-grey eyes and a burning desire to learn ancient secrets began to percolate throughout Asia and the South Seas. Then he showed up intermittently in Tibet, Borneo, and Java. Eventually the society-page watchers ceased caring about the man of mystery. Storm, however, wouldn't have cared even if he had known. Publicity was not important to him. Fame and glory would have mattered to him before but not now, not anymore.

His mysterious four-year circuit of the globe completed, Storm returned home to the United States. Bidding a good-bye to his home state of Michigan, he left behind his family's mansion in the care of the well-paid staff of servants. This sprawling castle-like structure would serve to be his refuge, should he need some time away from the world and his mission for reflection and solitude. He took root finally back in Miami, the place of so many of his selfish jaunts and debaucheries in the past, and purchased a large patch of disused land not far south along the eastern coast from the Pan American seaplane airport at Dinner Key. The land was soon converted to a private airfield, surrounded with a compound of buildings: laboratories, hangars, workshops, warehouses. He began to put out the word through many scientific societies and through friends he had made during his academia and subsequent journey around the world. Scientists, engineers, and mechanics from all walks of life were contacted with job offers and handsome paychecks in return for their participation in Storm's noble causes and utopian dreams. They came, along with others: thrill-seekers, adventurers... anyone with the drive to help the world and the struggling members of mankind, anyone who wanted to make a difference in the world. Anyone who wanted to help was welcome to join the cause.

Soon, with the new airfield and complex finalized and a capable and skilled team assembled, a sign was hung on the fence by the front gate of the compound:

MIAMI AERODROME:
RESEARCH AND DEVELOPMENT LABORATORIES

Beneath this title, in smaller print, the sign read:

C. STORM & ASSOCIATES
TROUBLESHOOTERS

The passenger on board the *Zephyr* smiled as he read the last few documents. These were files based upon the widely-known events that had brought Storm once again to the public eye and which were making him into a hero of sensational proportions

The first file was a write-up of an incident wherein an ocean liner in the North Atlantic Ocean had caught on fire. Many of the lifeboats had burned, and the passengers found themselves in a horrible situation: they were faced with the choice of either freezing to death in the icy and black nighttime waters or stay aboard and roast to death in the firestorm that was slowly devouring the ship. Storm and his team had been the first on the scene and had begun rescue operations, loading survivors into seaplanes for transport and fighting the growing blaze aboard the ship while rescuing those caught there. Once the rescue ships had shown up, the independent troubleshooters had continued to assist them in the rescue and salvage. By the time it was all over, they had left the scene. The rescue teams and the survivors of the accident praised their mysterious saviors without ever knowing who they had been. That was the first recorded incident of Clifton Storm's involvement in dangerous adventures.

The second recorded incident occurred when a group of scoundrels had robbed a bank in Tampa, Florida. The group hadn't just simply robbed the bank; they had coldly slaughtered everyone inside. A large number of men wearing gas masks and some kind of body armor had entered the bank: they locked the doors and shot the guards, afterward opening up tanks of lethal chemical vapors within the building. Soon, everyone had died inside but the robbers, who filled their loot sacks to bursting capacity from the money and valuables in the vaults. Outside, the police were powerless to stop the robbers. Between the body armor and the gas they were using, the criminals had the upper-hand. Meanwhile, a small and armed airship had arrived on the bank's roof and the looters began loading the stolen cash on board the craft.

Storm and a group of his assistants had arrived by plane and autogiro, and they succeeded in driving the criminals away. The adventurers had followed the group toward their hideout in the countryside, eventually forcing the airship down. The looters, however, did not give up without a fight, and what erupted then was nothing short of a small-scale war. The MARDL airplane provided cover for Storm and his allies as they landed in their autogiro and fought back hard against the heavily-armed gangsters on the ground. A few of the troubleshooters had been injured, one seriously so, and even Storm himself took a bullet. By the time the smoke cleared, however, the vigilantes had emerged from the battle victorious. The police had arrived soon after it was over to find members of the huge gang dead, injured, or shackled. Many citizens had lost their lives during the daring raid, but the criminals had been brought to justice and the money returned. The press, after getting wind of the adventurer's involvement with the incident, began calling Storm "Challenger" due to his team's brave flights into mysterious and dangerous events.

The final piece concerned the rescue of the hijacked airship, the *Goliath*. The passenger knew the details of this incident quite well, and so he skimmed over the information within this particular file. When he was done the passenger closed the files, arranging them carefully to nestle within their envelope once again, and closed the dossier fully.

His body and mind finally relaxing from his biographical study and the trance he'd been under, the passenger leaned back and closed his hard blue eyes. The events inside the collected files and notes showed the passenger the motives behind Storm's "mystery man" façade and helped to explain the facets that drove the man to create his troubleshooting team and the Miami Aerodrome Research and Development Laboratories.

The rest of the assignment was up to the passenger now. He knew that his instructions may not be met favorably and that he might be resisted. Outside the window, the *Zephyr's* whistle blew a long and lonely note through the dark air of the night, and the passenger smiled to himself: it was a shame that his abilities didn't extend to foretelling the future, as well.

CHAPTER 18: REUNIONS

The hostages were surprised at the direction in which they had been led. They had been following the river while searching from the air, but Richard Stein was now leading them eastward, deeper into the jungle. They followed the slightest path after a long time of trudging through the green hell of the jungle, and eventually this path converged with others and joined a larger dirt road that snaked through the jungle. Other paths and roads branched off in numerous directions, and it soon became apparent that beneath the canopy of the jungle trees the Villalobos Brothers and their men had carved a confusing system of routes that eventually led to their compound. Stein, however, had no problem following the treacherous winding system of trails.

After nearly two hours of walking, the group finally reached the main gates of the Villalobos compound. The guards positioned there were wary, but after a brief coded exchange in Spanish the gates opened to admit Stein and his prisoners. Soon more guards approached and covered the hostages with their weapons while Stein went on by himself to Jorge and Esteban Villalobos' private quarters.

Several minutes later, Richard Stein returned with the Brothers. They ignored J. Gordon Tolliver for the moment while they observed Willy, Skids, and Brock.

Smoothly, Esteban grinned. "Twice now you have slipped through our grasp, but now there is nowhere to run. I'm afraid there will be no escape for you this time, my friends. Now…," he turned to Stein. "Where is their leader?"

"Dead," said Stein proudly, "at the bottom of the valley."

Jorge Villalobos stepped forward toward Stein threateningly. "You were to bring them all here alive," he growled, eyes gleaming like a predator. "All of them."

"Storm was a thorn in my side," Stein defended. "I was tired of him and he made a move, so excuse me for drilling him myself. You would have done the same."

"Jorge is right," Esteban said, turning on Stein. "You disobeyed our orders..."

"Disobeyed your orders?!" Stein said incredulously. "Listen: you two aren't my bosses. I don't have to take orders from you. If anything, you should take orders from *me*; if it weren't for me you'd still be waging piddling little turf wars with the other tin-pot guerillas on this Godforsaken island. You certainly wouldn't be where you are now. You're about to hold the whole island in your hands and you know it's because of me."

For a moment there was an immense tension between the three men. Brock and Skids exchanged glances, while Willy looked on, ever alert to a moment they could use to turn toward their advantage. The situation, however, had provided no glimmer of hope so far, and they were covered by deadly weapons and watchful eyes the whole time.

Finally, suave Esteban waved his hand dismissively. "Gentlemen," he said, "There is no need to argue amongst ourselves right now. This is a time of celebration, of reunions." He turned toward Tolliver but spoke to his guards. "Take our guests here to their lodgings and keep a close eye on them. And you, *Señor* Stein, can go visit your lovely bride-to-be. Leave Jorge and me here with *Señor* Tolliver."

As Stein left the group, Tolliver glowered at his back. Jorge Villalobos grinned at the businessman, ugly teeth gleaming in the tropical sunlight. "Your friend Richard is a feisty one, Tolliver..."

"He's no friend of mine, not any more than the two of you are," Tolliver retorted. "He's certainly not my future son-in-law anymore now, either." His disgust was audible. "Now where the hell is my daughter?" he demanded.

Esteban laughed. "*Señor*, you will see her soon enough. But first..." He draped an arm over Tolliver's shoulder and they began to walk further into the compound, "...first we will make you a final offer. You took a chance on your daughter's life by seeking help. You are lucky that we did not harm her because of this transgression. We have killed for less."

Jorge grinned at the tycoon again. "Keep paying, Tolliver. Keep your daughter alive."

Indecision and fear were once again coursing through J. Gordon

Tolliver. He was funding an army now, perhaps even aiding them in expanding their conquests. If he kept paying, Kate would live (*if she's even still alive*, he thought feverishly), but how many more would be oppressed, enslaved, or even killed?

Katherine Tolliver's eyes hurt.

Ever since Esteban Villalobos had told her everything, she had been crying. She felt utterly defeated and fatigued. But even more than that, she felt betrayed. Her own father had funded the Villalobos Brothers, given them the money that they were using to construct some monstrous super-warplane. The money had gone towards the arming of what had swiftly become one of the most powerful guerrilla organizations in the world. True, the Brothers' group was tiny but it was now strong and deadly, hell-bent on ruling the island, then perhaps the region, then maybe even more…

She had managed to forgive her father somewhat. After all, he had tried to stop the funding (which had led to her imprisonment, unfortunately), and he had continued rebelling against the guerrillas and had sought help. By now, however, the hope of rescue would have been ended, all because of Stein's betrayal.

She would have absolutely no forgiveness for Richard Stein.

The man she once loved… whom she thought loved her… had used her, instead. He had been the one to tip off the Villalobos Brothers about her father's project, the one who had stolen the plans for the Paragon for his own use and for the Brothers'. He had helped the Villalobos Brothers in kidnapping her, and now he was sabotaging the rescue mission.

Her heart was filled with bitter rage… so much that when her cell door suddenly opened and Richard Stein filled the doorway it seemed as if she had summoned him with her pure, ferocious hatred.

He had showered in the compound's bath-house, had shaved and put on clean clothes and stood now in stark contrast to the sweating and filthy captive young woman that was chained before him. He regarded her oddly, as though she were a specimen on a slide and was to be examined with detached and unsympathetic eyes. Calmly, he ate an orange.

"Take her shackles off," he finally commanded the guard that stood at his side.

Kate was unchained, but neither man helped her to her feet, and so she stood herself up on her weak and cramped legs, holding the metal pole in the center of her cell for support.

"Orange slice?" he offered, holding the piece of fruit out to her. Although her mouth watered at the thought of the juicy piece of fruit, she slapped his hand away. Stein stared at her, a mock frown upon his face.

"I don't want anything from you." Kate's voice was icy.

Stein removed another orange slice and took a bite. "You realize, don't you, that the way you treat me now will affect what happens to you in the long run, right?" He took another bite. "I'd suggest that you be very, very careful, Kate."

"Why?" she asked. "Why did you do it? For money? Do they promise you power? Why?"

"Why, I did it for you, Kate. For us." He looked at her innocently.

"Us?" she cried. "Are you out of your mind, Richard?"

"But you deserve so much more than I could give you, sweetheart. With the money I have now- and the money I'll have soon- I can give you those things."

Kate scoffed. "Face it, Richard," she said after a moment of silence, "you're only saying those things in some lame attempt to put yourself in my good graces after doing all this to my father and me. As the saying goes..." and here she smiled grimly, "you want to have your cake and eat it, too. Well, you can forget about me. I'm not a dupe, and I won't fall for it. Go ahead and eat that cake, Richard. I hope you choke on it." Her grin was now defiant.

Stein swung his hand hard. The slap was sudden, powerful, but instead of crumbling as he had predicted, Kate caught the pole and lunged back at him. In her right hand was something gleaming... the shard of the shattered whiskey bottle she had kept hidden.

With a downward slash, she swung for Richard Stein's face. He was caught off guard but leaned back. The swing sliced through the flesh of his shoulder but he caught her hand at her second flashing strike. He gripped Kate's wrist and arm, bending it painfully until she dropped the piece of glass.

The guards had come forward into the cell, and Stein whirled and pushed Kate into them. His shoulder was oozing blood, but the fury in his eyes defied the pain she had wrought on him. He drew back his hand in a fist.

Katherine Tolliver thought he would strike her again and she prepared for another blow, but it did not come. Stein only glared hatefully at her.

"You'd better start praying that 'Daddy' keeps paying the Brothers," he snarled. "If he doesn't... then you'll surely be wolf-food." Then to the guards: "Chain this animal back up."

Kate struggled against the captors' rough hands, but it was no use. Shackled again to the pole she watched as the guards left the cell. She expected the door to close, but it did not. Instead, it filled with new faces: Esteban and Jorge Villalobos, and with them was her father.

"Daddy…" she said flatly, unsure of what to think of this reunion. Tolliver could only look down at the ground after glancing at her, his face awash with despair, fear, guilt.

"Your last chance, *Señor*," Esteban said smoothly.

Tolliver stood frozen, unsure of what to do. Jorge drew a pistol and pointed it at Kate's huddled form. He uttered only a single word to Tolliver:

"Decide."

CHAPTER 19: BLOOD SPORT

At that very moment, in another cell-shed nearby, Willy Avis and Skids crouched on the dirt floor. They too were chained to a pole in the center of their shed, but they weren't alone. Against one wall, chained and shackled at the arms, legs, waist, and even neck, was Brock Thurman.

His head had been lolling, unconscious. Suddenly he gave out a groan. Instinctively he tried to move his hand to touch the egg-sized lump that had formed on the back of his hairless head. The shackles, however, held his arm securely to the wall-supports, and he could not reach his head. His eyes opened slowly and squinted, and he looked about the cell groggily.

When the trio had been led away by the Villalobos' guards after they arrived at the camp, they had remained quiet and stoic. To attempt an escape at that time would have been foolish as several guns had been trained on them at all times, and they had no weapons of their own.

They had been led across the compound and towards the prison sheds when Brock had spied something that had made him livid with rage. A teenage girl- thin, bruised, and hollow-eyed- had been carrying a tray of food to a group of soldiers sitting at a long, rough table. One of the guerrillas groped at her, and she stepped away. The leering soldier had gotten up and knocked the plate of food from her hands, then pulled her to him lustily. The girl had struggled weakly in his grip.

Burning with rage, Brock had knocked aside one of the guards leading the trio and had launched himself toward the guard holding the girl. The soldier had dropped the girl, who promptly had then gotten up and fled, and reached for his sidearm. Before he could un-holster his weapon, Brock had savagely punched him, bursting the soldier's nose with his gigantic fist.

The guard had fallen with a whimper, but others had leaped up to swarm the former circus strongman. Willy and Skids had only been able to watch helplessly, their armed escorts never took their eyes- or their guns- off of their prisoners.

For a few moments, Brock had been able to hold his own against the group, swinging his massive arms like a whirling engine of punishment. Wherever his block-like fists had sledged, a soldier had fallen. One lithe and nimble attacker had leaped up to attempt a choke-hold on the brawler's neck; Brock had simply reached back and thrown the man off between the blows he dealt to the others.

Combatants had kept adding to the scuffle, though, and Brock had finally fallen under the weight of the pile of soldiers. The guard whom Brock had originally knocked aside rained furious blows upon the back of his head using the butt of his rifle, and eventually the strongman had lost consciousness. He had been carried by the soldiers (those who had still been able to do so) to the cell where he was now chained, securely fastened to the wall by thick and stout towing-chains.

"How're ya' feelin'?" queried Skids to Brock, without his usual hint of sarcasm.

"I'll live," grunted the big man.

Skids adjusted his cramped frame. "That's good. All those knocks to the head probably would've killed anybody else."

"How long have I been out?"

"Not long," Willy answered soberly. "With all that head trauma, we figured you'd be out for a long time." He managed to smile. "You're a tough one, kid."

Brock lowered his head. "I don't feel too tough." Then without looking at his companions: "What about Cliff?" It was the first the three had spoken of their leader since they left their encampment in the clearing by the valley. The question hung heavily in the air around the captives.

"Willy…" Skids said quietly. "Do you think that he could've made it?"

The mechanic shook his head slowly. "Not being shot at point-blank range like that. And whatever Stein saw when he looked over the edge… whatever it was, he seemed pretty confident."

The two other men exchanged looks; Brock and Skids were fully aware of the almost father-son relationship that Storm and Willy had. As tough as his loss was for them, for Willy Avis the despair must have been tenfold.

The silence hung over them thickly. Finally, Brock spoke. "When I get my hands on that traitor, he's gonna wish he'd died in that stupid pumpkin-patch crash…"

"You mean *if* you ever get your hands on him," Willy interrupted. "We're outnumbered and being watched all the time here." His voice was bitter. "Let's face it, boys… unless a miracle comes along, we're sunk."

The three men lapsed again into silence. The only sound they could hear outside was the endless droning of the heat-bugs and cicadas.

"Decide," Jorge Villalobos repeated. He cocked his pistol for emphasis.

J. Gordon Tolliver looked beyond the barrel, at the wide blue eyes of his daughter. Katherine, meanwhile, was looking into his own eyes without fear and was paying no attention to the pistol in Jorge's hand.

"Don't do it, Daddy," she said defiantly.

Tolliver's mind was in utter turmoil. Should he continue to pay these butchers, continue to fund an army growing ever more powerful and brutal? That seemed like the thing he should do… to keep Kate alive, he had to pay them, had to keep being the Villalobos Brothers' puppet. But the more he looked into his daughter's eyes, the more he looked at the murderous intent on the devilish face of their captors, the more a creeping feeling became known to him.

If he kept paying them, Kate would live. The Villalobos Brothers had assured him that he had their word… but how good was that word? He knew, deep inside, that they would never let her go free. They would keep her a prisoner, probably keep her in the same filthy conditions and all the while would use her for leverage. He would keep paying them while she suffered. And then, eventually, the Villalobos Brothers would either bleed him dry of all his funds or just outgrow their need for his payments, and then… would they return Kate to him? No. They would either kill her anyway or keep her for whatever filthy purposes they wished. It made his stomach turn.

At last, then, he knew his answer to them. At least this way they would hopefully shoot them both. This way would hopefully be a quicker end to the suffering.

"Go to hell," he spat, and lunged at Jorge, swinging his fist at the warlord's face.

But Tolliver was older, slower than he had given himself. Jorge Villalobos stepped back, and Tolliver was thrown off balance by his missed punch.

Esteban's foot flashed out, striking Tolliver in the side of the left knee. The tycoon felt a sickening crunch as his leg buckled. He collapsed.

Katherine Tolliver screamed, helpless to assist her father as Jorge began stomping and kicking at his prone form. Esteban glared down at the huddled form, preferring not to dirty himself with combat any further than he had to. He finally held out his cane to hold back Jorge, who continued to gaze hatefully at Tolliver with crazed eyes.

Esteban crouched down near Tolliver's defeated form. "If you've attempted this as some sort of bravado, some kind of gambit to earn you and your daughter a merciful death, then it has been a wasted effort," he purred. "The two of you, as well as your friends from America, will soon find that we have no mercy for anyone, especially those who resist us." He looked at Katherine. "You will all be our sport," he said with a grin.

Kate's eyes grew wide, but she continued glaring at the two brothers.

Esteban and Jorge Villalobos left the cell, instructing their pair of guards to chain J. Gordon Tolliver to the pole along with his daughter. After that they left, leaving the two captives alone with the clang of the cell door.

Tolliver turned his bloodied and bruised face toward Kate. Her tear-stained face stared back. In it, Tolliver saw his little girl and his deceased wife, as well as all the wrong he had done and all he would never make right. He saw the end of their world. "I'm sorry," he whispered to her. He began to sob gently.

Kate pulled her father to her and rested his head on her shoulder as he continued to cry remorsefully.

Time seemed to pass eternally slow for the captives. The day grew longer and hotter. Slowly, the quiet murmur of the militia grew. By the time the light from the late afternoon sun came slanting into the cell sheds, it was evident that some kind of gathering was taking shape outside, as voices and footsteps could be heard shuffling, and conversations began to babble around them. Spirits were high, and the revelers sounded confident and swaggering.

It was a pre-war party.

Shortly after the public-address system was tested, the prisoners were gathered from their cells. Tolliver and Kate were led to join Brock, Willy, and Skids and together they were marched toward the center of the compound. They weren't chained or shackled, but the guns of their captors were trained on them closely. At any sudden movement from the prisoners, they would be shot dead. The guards were uneasy after the savage show of strength from Brock earlier, and they called to others for assistance. On the left side of the prisoners a youngish guard fell into step with them and drew his pistol: it was the would-be rapist of Katherine Tolliver, who was eager to get back into the good graces of his employers. He leered at Kate from behind the bandages on his face. A shabbily-dressed soldier, cap pulled low over his eyes to meet his upturned collar, strode in from the right in response to his comrades' call for help. He also drew his pistol and trained the automatic on the captives as they continued their march toward the center point of the compound.

They were led to the pit in the center of the Villalobos Brothers' base. The entire guerilla force had turned out to watch what would take place at this morale-boosting meeting, and they hooted and cheered when the group of prisoners appeared.

"What's going on?" asked Skids. Kate told him of the pit of bones, and of the starved wolves and the helpless prisoner she had seen being devoured by them. "But there are five of us," he responded. "I'm sure that we could hold our own against three wolves."

In response, Kate pointed to the guard towers. "Apparently they think so, too." Following her indication, her captive companions saw the posted guards there holding high-powered hunting rifles.

"It's a game stacked in their favor," Willy said quietly. "One way or another, we lose."

They were walked to the edge of the pit and lined up along it. At their left by Kate stood the youngish guard with the bandaged face; on their right, by Willy, stood the dirty-looking guard in the cap. Behind the prisoners were the four other guards who had led them out. Off to the group's left the militia had gathered in a half-circle, at the center of which was a raised platform. Upon it stood Jorge Villalobos with his leashed wolves, along with a smug Richard Stein. Brock and Skids were shocked when they saw that standing next to Stein was Panza, the chief of police, and they glared at the source of their earlier betrayal as they told Willy who he was and of his part in their ambush.

"Hola, friends," said Jorge Villalobos into the microphone and over the loudspeakers. "I see you have met our chief of police here before." He laughed.

Panza joined in his own laughter and took the microphone. "Oh yes," he said, "I have met some of you... twice, in fact." He removed the black-

"Jorge...led his starving beasts to the shed..."

rimmed spectacles he wore and tugged at his beard and nose, fakes which promptly came off. Beneath this disguise, he was revealed... as Esteban Villalobos.

The crowd erupted into laughter at the face of the prisoners, who looked on with shocked expressions. They had been duped, as had everyone on La Isla de Sangre. The new police chief in Templo del Sol had been their number one public enemy the entire time.

"Forgive me, my friends, but I could not resist seeing your face once you realized my ruse," Esteban continued. He nodded to Jorge, who left the platform and led his starving beasts to the shed at the edge of the pit. That shed concealed the tunnel that would lead them down to the pit...

"Now, soldiers of Villalobos," Esteban continued. "Today we prepare for an onslaught. We take what is ours. Today, we teach the king to fear us. There is nothing... nothing that will stop us from our strike on the cowards of Templo Del Sol. We will start with Jorge and his wolves today, and from there we will press onward. We will make the very rivers of La Isla de Sangre run red with the blood of those who would oppose us, and we will punish those who have resisted us for so long..." He paused to face the prisoners. "And we will start with you," he said and pointed toward the prisoners. On the warlord's face was an evil and lupine smile that chilled their blood.

Behind them, the guards prepared to push the prisoners into the pit of slaughter, while Esteban Villalobos raised his hand to signal their doom...

CHAPTER 20: RAID

The signal never came.

Behind the prisoners and their guards, the Villalobos' armory suddenly exploded. The large building had housed the weapons and many of the land vehicles of the guerrilla army; now, it seemed as if it leaped off of its foundation and blossomed into a raging fireball. Waves of smoke and soot washed towards all areas of the compound, and a towering column of smoke rose into the jungle sky as the ground shook from the explosion. In that moment, chaos and confusion broke out and reigned for every person in the compound.

Every person but one.

The dirtily-attired soldier standing by the prisoners burst into action. He spun to face their other guards, a second pistol appearing in his left hand… a Mauser. With rapid, accurate shots he pumped lead from both pistols into the other guards. The attack was swift and decisive; the soldier with the bandaged face went down, as did the other four who had no chance to even draw their weapons as the bullets struck home.

"Come on, follow me!" the shabby guard shouted to the prisoners as he passed his right-hand pistol to Willy. No longer slouching, his face was fully revealed.

"Cliff!" shouted Brock in recognition. The group was stunned by the surreal- though welcome- turn of events, but they snapped out of it at Storm's barked order. Following him, they sprinted from the pit's edge, while the panicking soldiers around them raced around still blinded by the confusion of the explosion.

A second explosion shook the ground as another batch of munitions burst in the flaming armory. The soldiers scurried about: some rushed toward the wrecked building in some half-mad desire to put out the boiling flames; some of them ran for cover from the flying debris and wreckage. Some could only stand dumbly as they tried to figure out what was going on, while a few soldiers who had been close to the explosions were engulfed in flames and crazily running, trying to extinguish their torched bodies. None of the militia seemed to notice Storm and the fleeing line of prisoners.

Only Esteban Villalobos, still rooted to the podium on the speaking platform, saw them. He gripped the microphone still, his knuckles white with fear and outrage. He saw Storm and the group disappear around the corner of the barracks and he knew then what happened, what had transpired to shake his plans.

Richard Stein had crouched instinctively behind Esteban when the first explosion rocked the compound; Esteban yanked the test pilot to his feet by the front of his shirt. "Who was that?!" he screamed into Stein's face. "Was that him? Was that Storm?!"

"I-it must've been… It couldn't have been…" Stein babbled. "I thought… I mean, I knew he was dead… He had to be, I shot him… a-at point-blank range…"

Esteban threw him aside. "Well, apparently he got better!" he screamed at Stein. He was furious. He had to have order, he thought, he had to get things under control and stop the escapees and their savior. He snatched the microphone to his face and began screaming orders over the PA system.

Storm led the prisoners through a course that he had predetermined while planning their escape; he had done so hastily and was hoping his memory of the route was correct. The serpentine course wound between the compound's buildings, which provided cover for them from the main square. Around them, chaos continued to hold sway over the Brothers' men and soldiers ran in all directions, but the prisoners managed to stay out of sight as much as possible.

"Wait!" Katherine Tolliver cried. She had seen a furtive, confused figure between the barracks and kitchen buildings. "That was Rosa; we need to bring her with us!"

Storm and the others stopped peered around the corner. The hollow-eyed girl stood several yards away, stood still as though entranced and rooted to the spot. A dull fear shone on her face as she watched the tumult around her.

"I got her," rumbled Brock, and he shouldered past the group and raced toward the girl. Her eyes flared to life as she recognized the big man who had tried to come to her aid hours before. He waved to Rosa to follow, but the sudden movement as she approached him alerted a trio of soldiers. They aimed their submachine guns.

Brock scooped the girl up and raced back toward his friends as the soldiers opened fire. They underestimated the big man's nimbleness and speed, though, and their bullets sprayed wide. As Brock and Rosa disappeared into the alley the trio of soldiers broke into a run to follow the pair.

At the other end of the alley, Storm and Willy opened up cover fire from their pistols. The soldiers were too far away for their shots to be accurate, but they scurried for cover from the shots. Once out of sight, however, they called to their comrades and soon the word spread from man to man: the escaping prisoners had been spotted.

"We're almost there, come on!" Storm urged as they ran, "They're calling help!"

He led them away from the buildings to a stand of trees in a remote corner of the compound. There, among the tangled foliage, the ground sloped down gently to form a natural bowl. Into this pit the group leaped; at the bottom, a tarpaulin lay carefully hidden and covered in branches. Storm whipped this camouflage back to reveal a small stash of weapons he had placed there earlier. Among the hidden guns was a fat-barreled drum-fed Lewis machine gun. Brock hefted the gun as though it was a tin toy and grinned. It was one of the muscle-man's favorite weapons.

"Aw, Cliff, you shouldn't have!" he chuckled.

As Brock began setting up the gun's tripod on the rim of the pit, Storm began passing the weapons around to the others, swiftly explaining to Kate the operation of her gun. The only person who didn't have a weapon was Rosa, who slumped dazedly against the back wall of the pit. Her expression was still numb, shell-shocked by the treatment of La Isla de Sangre's criminal groups and she curled into a fetal position.

Readying his own Tommy gun at the forward edge, Skids tried to stammer out questions to their newly resurrected leader. "Cliff... how... what's...?"

"I'll tell you later," Storm said as he got into position beside him. "For now, we need to hold these guys off!"

As if on cue, the two pursuing soldiers rounded the corner of the nearest building and halted. As the first fatigue-clad warrior appeared, the group in the pit held still, hoping to go unnoticed for as long as possible. The third soldier to appear around the corner, however, chanced to look right at the group. At his cry of alarm, the other shifted their gaze to spot them too. They raised their weapons to fire…

A volley of fire from Storm and his companions cut into the soldiers and two went down amidst a bloody spray. The soldier who spotted them first had fallen back to the corner of the building as his call for help was answered, though, and this newly arrived group of soldiers opened fire on the escapees from their cover spots at the barracks. The volley from the guerrillas forced their targets to duck into the pit as bullets whizzed over their heads and clattered among the trees around them.

But this didn't last long. The soldiers received an answer to their shots from Brock's Lewis gun. The burst of lead forced them to seek shelter back around the corners again. But now other soldiers were being led in opposite directions, and these appeared at the corners of the buildings on either side of the prisoners' pit.

Storm caught a glimpse of the group on their right. "They're trying to flank us! Spread your fire!" he barked. He and Skids took the group of new attackers on their right while Willy and Tolliver took care of the left-hand soldiers. The original group of soldiers, positioned behind the corner toward the prisoners' middle field of fire, began to advance once again; Brock and Katherine Tolliver set their weapons' sights on them.

A furious firefight erupted then, and Storm and his group fought as bravely and as fiercely as they could to turn their attackers away. Every time a soldier popped from cover behind a rock, tree, or building corner they were met with deadly accurate fire from the pit, and Storm lobbed many of his specially designed high-explosive grenades at the advancing enemies. But as many soldiers were felled by the heroes' bullets and bombs, just as many seemed to take their place. The Villalobos' reinforcements seemed to be growing more and more assured with each return shot, and soon it was evident that they were working their way ever closer to the pit. The situation was growing grimmer for the escapees by the second.

A soldier appeared on the right, closer than the others, and Storm saw him yank the pin from a hand grenade. As he drew back his arm to throw the explosive, Storm steadied his Tommy gun and ripped off a quick burst, tearing into the soldier's chest. The would-be grenadier stopped in his tracks, eyes wide, as the grenade slipped from his hand and to the ground. His body fell backward as the grenade exploded with a thunderous roar, causing the other soldiers and their quarry alike to duck for cover.

"This is turning into the Alamo, Cliff!" yelled Skids over the roar of the gunfire. "How much longer are we going to have to hold out?"

Storm considered the answer himself. They would be running out of ammunition soon, and the militia was gaining ground and coming closer to their defended position. He had to buy more time.

From the utility harness beneath his fatigue jacket, he pulled a grenade shaped like a ball. "Sonic!" he barked at his companions as he pulled the grenade's pin.

"Cover your ears," Skids told Rosa and the Tollivers as Storm threw the device. All of the members of the group clapped their hands to their heads as he lobbed the grenade upwards toward a spot over an advancing group of Villalobos soldiers. There, at the apex of Storm's throw, it burst.

The grenade was not explosive; instead it operated using compressed air. As the grenade's outer shell broke open with a loud "pop" sound, the air around it was filled suddenly with cunningly constructed thin metal spiral shapes. These flew out of the popping grenade device to flutter downward slowly, like dropped feathers. Unlike feathers, however, they were not silent. As they floated down, the air passing over the tiny spiraled slivers made a shrieking whistling sound. Suddenly everywhere above and around the soldiers was filled with the ear-splitting whistles and the Villalobos' men suddenly found it hard to do anything but experience intense ear-aches. A few of the rebels even dropped to their knees in agony as their comrades scurried for cover away from the hideous sounds.

Storm knew that the tricks he held, such as the sonic grenades, would keep the enemies at bay for only a short time. Sooner or later, they would run out of tricks and ammunition and the group in the hole would be like sitting ducks to the blood-thirsty guerillas. He began to curse himself for pushing his luck so far, for endangering the others so much with his escape scheme. He wondered how long it would be before their luck would run out...

And then suddenly it happened... the miracle that Storm had been banking on.

A hundred feet away, a truck burst through the front gate of the compound. Its front end was outfitted with a sturdy battering ram, and a group of men rode in the back. They cut down the guards posted at the gate with their own machine gun fire. Behind the truck followed five more of the vehicles and with them were dozens of men, both on foot and in the vehicles. The men were clad in dark blue uniforms... police. And leading the charge, revolver in hand, was Detective Anando Del Rio.

The newly-arrived lawmen poured into the Villalobos compound, and the soldiers found they were suddenly becoming outgunned as they faced the withering fire of the unexpected blue-clad newcomers. The confronted soldiers began a slow retreat, a sudden fear gripping them. They were being defeated.

Esteban and Jorge Villalobos, along with Richard Stein, had been making their way across the compound toward the battle when they heard the commotion of the front gate being breached over the sounds of gunfire. From a distance, they saw the flood of police that was raiding their compound. Esteban turned to his brother.

"*Es tiempo para irse,*" he said. "It is time to go."

Jorge dropped the leashes on his wolves, and the beasts looked blankly about them, unsure of what to do. Richard Stein's face echoed that look as the brothers turned and strode toward the other direction, toward a car parked outside their quarters.

"Wait," he called, hurrying to catch up with them. "Wait, where are we going?"

"'We' are going nowhere," said Esteban, who snapped his fingers suddenly. Jorge calmly turned around and shot Stein in the leg with one of his revolvers. The bullet ripped through the test pilot's left thigh. The wolves, startled by the shot, ran frantically away as Stein crumpled in pain. He held his bloody leg and cursed while the brothers continued toward the vehicle. Twenty feet away, Esteban called to him as he prepared to climb into the car with Jorge.

"You have outlived your purpose, and have now become useless to us. There is no room for uselessness in our organization." He got in and slammed the door as Jorge started the engine and the auto shot away in a cloud of red-tinged dust, leaving Stein bleeding and shocked on the ground.

Although the investigators missed their departure, it didn't take long for the remaining soldiers of the Villalobos militia to discover that their leaders had abandoned them. Feeling suddenly betrayed and defeated, they finally surrendered to the police forces. The lawmen had been assembled by Del Rio from every available and trustworthy policeman from every town on La Isla de Sangre. How they had come to find the Villalobos's hidden base would have to remain a mystery to the former captives for now, but they were grateful that their reinforcements had shown up in the nick of time the way they had.

Storm caught up with Del Rio in the center of the compound near the slaughter-pit, where all the members of the beaten guerrilla group had been assembled. Nearby, medics were tending to Katherine and J. Gordon Tolliver.

The adventurer looked around after a moment of discussion with Del Rio. "Wait… we're missing someone," he said to the investigator. "The Brothers… where are they?"

"We have yet to flush them out of their hole, but we will find them. My men are combing the place now." Del Rio was confident. The raid had been easy and over quickly.

"You won't find them here anymore, *Señor*," one of the arrested soldiers nearby called to them. "They've saved themselves and left us to be put away. I saw them leave. They are cowards."

Storm and Del Rio were alarmed at this. "Where'd they go?" Storm asked, stepping closer to the soldier who spoke.

"To the *Goddess… La Diosa De La Muerte*," he replied, pointing to the previously unseen tire tracks in the blood-red clay. They led through a small open gate and into a path in the jungle foliage beyond the compound fence.

They looked at the prisoner, who grinned evilly… he was ready and happy to betray his own betrayers. Storm turned to Del Rio. "They're making a break for it. My men and I can go after them," he said. "Can you and yours…"

"*Si*," Del Rio interrupted, "we have it under control here. Take one of our vehicles." He jerked his head toward the parked trucks.

Storm turned to his men. "These guys aren't going out without taking a bunch of people with them. Willy, Brock: you're coming with me. Skids, get back to our camp and get the *Witch* up into the air, then get right back to this area as quickly as possible. We're going to try and stop their plane from launching. If we don't and it leaves the ground, then keep after it. Follow it, and if it leaves the valley. I want you to blow it out of the sky. If we've failed, then do everything you can to stop it from getting back to civilization."

Skids swallowed and nodded gravely. He knew what his friend and boss meant without him having to say it: "…even if we're on board."

Richard Stein hobbled around the corner of one of the compound's buildings, and then quickly ducked back behind it. After a moment, he peeked around the corner and it was obvious he had not been spotted by anyone. Around that corner, Clifton Storm and his men were rapidly discussing plans. Stein glared at the troubleshooter's back with an icy, murderous stare. He wasn't sure how Storm had been able to survive those shots, and he really didn't care now. He'd almost had it all, and now it was gone, thanks to Storm. All Stein wanted to do now was to take revenge on the troubleshooter for ruining what was to have been his ticket to wealth and power. He thirsted to watch Storm's death; he would make sure that he was dead for real this time. He tightened the rag tourniquet he had hastily tied around his thigh and checked the pistol he'd taken off a dead Villalobos soldier. He was ready now for his vengeance.

Clifton Storm and his crew were hastily making their way to one of the police trucks and Stein hurriedly limped from his hiding spot, advancing rapidly toward his unsuspecting target's back. Though injured and hobbled, Stein's resolve burned within him and made him swift and steady.

He was close enough now, and wouldn't miss this time. He raised his pistol, aiming between Storm's shoulder-blades, and his finger began to tighten on the trigger...

CHAPTER 21: SLAVES OF THE LOST CITY

A thunderous pistol shot cracked out, splitting the humid air and turning every head in the compound.

Storm and his three troubleshooters spun around, weapons at the ready. Before them stood Richard Stein, his pistol aimed at Storm. He was still and quiet as a statue until the pistol in his hand wavered, and then fell to the dirt. A ribbon of blood unfurled from his lips.

Stein's body collapsed like a rag doll and lay still; behind him stood Katherine Tolliver, a smoking automatic clenched in her hand.

Time seemed to stand still as the entire group- captured soldiers, policemen, Storm and his men- viewed the tableau. Kate stood over the body of the man she had once loved, and she looked ragged and nearly skeletal and so very, very tired.

Finally, she raised her eyes to meet Storm's own. "Go," she said.

He gave her a single terse nod, and the four adventurers turned away.

Skids and a police officer raced back through the jungle in the officer's truck toward the MARDL team's campsite from the previous night, while Storm, Brock, and Willy thundered through the jungle in their own truck, following the winding dirt path that the Villalobos Brothers had taken. Brock rode in the back, his Lewis gun at the ready for any surprise ambushes by Villalobos forces, while Storm drove and Willy rode shotgun. The trio did not speak to each other during the ride as each man harbored the same fears. They pictured the Villalobos Brothers and their super-plane, in a last spasm of conquering rage and defiance, as they rained down destruction and death upon the innocent people of the island. The streets of Templo Del Sol would fill with chaos, blood, and fire and the good people of the capitol city would pay for the troubleshooters' slowness and failure if they didn't stop them first.

Suddenly the path ahead of their truck burst out of the jungle, the foliage parting like a curtain for their passage, and below them a scene unfolded that seemed out of a lost world.

A panoramic view of the valley's head spread out before them. The view showed the adventurers a massive waterfall cascading from the rocky crags there, spilling down to the river far below. On a rocky plateau beside the falls was a fantastic, ancient city. Stone temples and spires seemed to dominate the streets, and all the structures and paving stones appeared to be an intricate patchwork of the island's blood-red clay and the obsidian-colored Skyrock. The ancient city was constructed in the style of the Incan Indians, but new and modern structures of stone, steel, aluminum, and wood had sprung up like cancerous growths within it.

Right next to the waterfall was the largest of the new structures, a combination power-plant and factory. This was connected to a huge water-wheel positioned in the fall's path, and behind the factory was a giant mound of the mined Skyrock. Not far from the huge factory building was a massive hangar fronted by a short runway. The hangar took up most of what appeared to have once been the city's gigantic central square, and many of the city's original structures had been demolished and hauled away or simply just knocked down haphazardly to make room for it. The gigantic doors of the hangar were open, but from the men's vantage-point the glimpse inside only revealed an impenetrably dark interior.

Along the perimeter of the ruined city were several guard tower-like structures as well, but these seemed to be deserted. There was one more building beside the hangar and factory plant, however. This appeared to be some kind of large roofed-in cattle pen, the doors of which were securely chained and locked.

There was no activity in the desecrated ancient city. It looked as though it were truly deserted.

Storm stopped the truck on a ledge that overlooked the scene. Were they too late? Had the Brothers already departed?

"Where is everybody?" asked Willy. The fear that they had failed had intensified.

Suddenly, a group of six soldiers appeared from within the hangar in the distance. One of these carried a backpack fitted with large canisters and a gun-like nozzle... a flamethrower. The other five men carried torches that they now lit from the flame at the tip of the fire-launching weapon. The group approached the pen-like structure, and a sudden wave of nausea swept over Storm as his eyes narrowed.

"The slaves...," he growled, "They're gonna burn them." He stamped the truck's accelerator pedal. The vehicle leaped into motion and rocketed down the final stretches of the path and down onto the plateau. Ahead, the soldiers turned, startled by the sudden appearance of the truck bearing down on them. All but the flamethrower-carrying man dropped their torches and reached for their weapons. The arsonist paid the truck no attention, and a searing tongue of fire soared from the weapon's nozzle, igniting the slave-pens. From within, the sounds of ragged screaming and shouting erupted.

Brock's Lewis gun blazed into fury; a staccato stream of lead flew over the roof of the truck and the deadly bullets tore into the flamethrower-soldier and his pack of canisters. Both the guerrilla and his tanks of chemicals burst into flame; he staggered away screaming and twisting, burning in the conflagration of the flamethrower's accelerant chemicals. He didn't get very far before collapsing into a wildly jerking, fiery heap.

The truck had closed the gap and was now directly before the others, and Storm swerved the vehicle into a pair of them. They were knocked aside by the armored truck's battering-ram like limp rag-dolls; the remaining three soldiers scattered. Storm slowed the truck as Willy leaped from the passenger-side. Tommy gun blazing, he cut down the three remaining would-be arsonists before they could get him in their sights. Meanwhile, Storm and Brock leaped out and to the aid of the trapped slaves inside the fiery hell that their holding-pens had become. The flames were licking higher up the outer walls, and starved, near-skeletal hands could be seen clawing frantically through any aperture in the cell-doors. They were going to be roasted alive.

Willy joined his two companions and they began to furiously tear at the doors of the pens. They would have to shoot out the locks and hope not to hit any captives within. Suddenly, movement at the hangar caught Storm's attention and the *Goddess of Death*, born from Tolliver's stolen Paragon plans, slowly emerged into the sunlight...

The police officer that Del Rio assigned to drive Skids back to the camp was a reckless daredevil who would've been right at home driving in the Indy 500. As Skids hung on for dear life, the grinning driver propelled their truck in a maniacal course through the jungle, sometimes following the path and other times disregarding it completely and plowing through the foliage like a wild beast.

When their vehicle finally reached the edge of the jungle it hit a large bump and seemed to soar out of the trees, landing crazily in the field. Ahead, Skids could see the planes and the camp, and let out a sigh of relief that nothing had been tampered with yet... and that his ride with the crazily-driving officer was over. He leaped out as the truck screeched to a halt in a cloud of dust beside the *Witch*.

"Thanks for the ride. Tell your boss you need a raise," he called out as he strapped on his helmet, "... and that you should get a desk job so you'll never have to drive again!" The driver replied with a broad grin and a thumbs-up gesture.

Leaping into the cockpit, Skids hit the electronic starter and disengaged the wheel-brakes. In a few moments the little black-and-red fighter plane was roaring into the sky, its compact yet powerful twin engines making a defiant scream in the late-afternoon air.

Skids banked the *Witch* sharply and turned her toward his destination. In his mind he urged the plane to produce more speed, hoping his arrival wouldn't be too late.

It took a moment or two for Storm to register the plane called the *Goddess of Death*, a moment for him to take it all in. In a way it reminded him of the Dornier DO-X, the much-maligned air-liner that had made headlines in previous years. Like the DO-X, the *Goddess* had a large, almost whale-shaped fuselage which narrowed toward the tail. The *Goddess*, like the other plane, also boasted a massive pair of wings at the top of the fuselage as well as a smaller pair at the bottom.

The similarities with the luxury airliner ended there, however: the huge plane before Storm fairly bristled with gun turrets, and the bottom "wings" weren't wings at all. These were thick platforms upon which were mounted more machine gun turrets as well as a massive howitzer cannon at the outside edges. The engines, too, were unusual: four gigantic radials were individually mounted on what appeared to be massive swiveling pivots, as though they could be pointed in any direction independently. These engines began to run, the massive propellers whirling and announcing the Brothers' imminent escape.

It wasn't hard for Storm to picture the weird aircraft hovering low in the sky, raining death and destruction down below, and he knew there probably wasn't much time before that image became a reality. He broke into a run toward it.

"Cliff!" Willy called after him.

Storm turned only for a moment. "Get those people out of there!" he called back before he spun again toward the plane, which seemed to shimmer in the slanting rays of the sun. As he got nearer to it, Storm could see that its surface was crisscrossed, the steel hull and wings were webbed with a glittering black substance... veins of pure Skyrock.

Just as his feet hit the asphalt of the runway the craft began to glow with a barely visible soft violet light, and it began to slowly rise into the air.

Storm surged the last few yards to the warplane and leaped toward the starboard-side landing gear, catching a tenuous hold of it as the craft rose. He scrambled for a better grip on the greased metal of the gear as the *Goddess* began to ascend more rapidly, her multiple engines roaring. Dwindling below, he could see the lost city and the Villalobos' hangar and factory, could see the flood of thin bodies as the freed slaves escaped from the fiery ruins of their holding-pens. He smiled grimly, silently congratulating Willy and Brock on the success of their efforts. Then he turned his attention to the task at hand: getting inside the plane. Looking up. He saw the recessed well of the landing gear above him and saw a thin door running along the well's ceiling. It was an access door for mid-flight repairs. Storm was examining the door and wondering how to get it open and whether he could fit through it when the sounds of grinding machinery surrounded him... the landing gear was being raised. If he didn't make it through the little door now he would be slowly crushed by the retracting mechanisms.

With his free hand he began pressing the steel hatch. It budged a little in the middle, but latches on the inside held it at either end and kept it firmly closed.

Constantly aware of the menace of the rising landing gear, Storm pushed harder, straining against the access door. Slowly the door bent, bowing further inward. With the gear now at a near-vertical angle beneath him he braced his feet against the massive wheel, and with both hands now he fought against the latched corners of the door. The gear still came up, and he now found he had to crouch in the shrinking space. He pushed and fought the door furiously, imagining the feeling of being crushed...

Suddenly, the latches inside snapped and the door flew inward.

Gripping the edges of the door's frame he pulled, raising himself into the plane. His chest and stomach seemed too wide and thick for the thin doorway, though. He was stuck, and his legs were threatened by the gear's rising. With a last effort, pushing with his arms and legs, he popped free and climbed through the hatch all the way. He rolled onto the floor of the plane's interior maintenance-space, soaking with sweat, as he heard the landing gear nestle home into the well below him.

CHAPTER 22:
TO KILL A GODDESS

Skids had swung the *Witch* in low over the trees at the edge of the lost city just in time to catch the massive super-plane lifting off the runway. He had popped the pursuit-plane's weapon pods open and, fingering the trigger, had centered the *Goddess of Death* in his sights.

Then he had caught sight of the lone, tiny figure dressed in dirty fatigues that had been hanging on to the landing gear and he had removed his finger from the trigger. Storm was on board, or at least was attempting to get on board and was trying to stop the plane now by himself. Skids' role had changed. Now knew he would have to follow the *Goddess of Death*, and should Storm fail he would have to try and shoot if down if it strayed too close to civilization.

Skids had swallowed hard. "C'mon, Cliff," he said to himself. "Don't make me have to shoot you down, too," as he had watched Storm's struggle to get inside.

Inside the maintenance-access area, Clifton Storm lay on his back, arms and legs still shaking from the effort of forcing the access door open and squeezing himself into the plane. He had drawn his trusty Mauser the moment he'd rolled onto the floor, but so far no one had come along yet. The gear well that Storm had climbed up into was located under the thick gunnery platform, and Storm was inside a tiny crawl space inside it. It was part of a system of access tunnels that connected the gunnery stations to the rest of the plane.

On his hands and knees he now began crawling toward the fuselage while keeping his pistol at the ready before him. As he passed them he noted that each gunnery station was empty… the Villalobos Brothers had been in a hurry and were flying the *Goddess* with less crew members than he thought. He began to think maybe they wouldn't be able to carry out their strike on the city after all...

That thought faded when he realized suddenly that the controls of each gun's nest was hooked up to a complicated system of gears and pistons. It was some kind of robotic control system, no doubt linked up with a remote station somewhere else in the plane. Tolliver hadn't mentioned that kind of set-up; no doubt this was one of the Villalobos Brothers' own crafty inventions, or perhaps it was Richard Stein's doing.

With a hardened resolve he crawled further into the aircraft...

At the rear of the plane, Jorge Villalobos struggled into a parachute. He disliked the *Goddess of Death*; indeed, he had a hatred of all airplanes. He saw no reason to trust any structure that tried to tempt fate and stay in the air, no matter what kind of system was being used to lift and push it. He resented the fact that he had to ride in the plane now, and wished he could have stayed on the ground. For a brief moment, he wondered what had become of the pet wolves he'd left behind, though not from any kindly concerns: he regretted having had to leave them after spending so much time honing their ferocity and blood-lust. To him they had been deadly weapons, assets to the Brothers' ferocious reputation and a terrifying symbol of their brothers' namesake.

He frowned suddenly. Outside the window, he had momentarily spotted a second shadow behind that of the massive super-plane's, silhouetted against the rocks and trees below. It blinked out... no, there it was again.

Racing to the other side of the plane, Jorge craned his head and peered out of the bubbled-window of a machine gun turret. A small black and crimson plane was following them, glinting in the late afternoon sun. He keyed the intercom as he brought the microphone up to his lips. "Brother, someone is following us! I'm cutting them down." He turned to unlatch the robotic control from the nearest .50 caliber turret.

"No," Esteban replied. "I've got it under control from here. You'll need to get up here to the cockpit, to be ready for when we reach the city."

Grunting in his frustration at not being able to do the killing himself, Jorge cast a last scornful glance at the pursuit craft, then turned to stalk forward toward the front of the plane.

Cautiously, Storm advanced through the center of the *Goddess of Death*. The interior was much more cramped than it appeared to be from

"...he crawled further into the aircraft..."

the outside, and Storm was constantly ready to stumble upon an occupied gun placement. His tensions seemed unwarranted, however. The gunnery stations in the aircraft's fuselage all seemed to be deserted.

Suddenly, the turrets all sprang to life at once as the robotic controls began to swing the guns into position. Several machine guns began hammering on the plane's starboard side, and Storm rushed to the nearest one and looked out of the window.

Behind the *Goddess of Death*, Storm could see the *Witch* weaving from side to side. Skids' expert piloting skills avoided the raking streams of hot lead and tracers coming from the *Goddess of Death*. He smiled slightly. Skids was doing everything in his power to stick with the escaping warlords. Storm was confident that if he failed, his number-one pilot would be able to bring the giant assault craft down.

He was determined, however, not to let the opportunity arise.

Swiftly covering the remaining fore area of the fuselage, Storm arrived at the spacious cockpit. Pressing himself against the corner he peered into it, taking it all in with a glance of his aviator's eyes before acting.

The space was large, but was occupied by only two men. In the pilot's seat was a man in a flying helmet who manipulated the controls, most of which resembled those of a standard passenger plane. An additional set of controls- which resembled a throttle- gave away the unusual nature of the aircraft. As Storm watched, the pilot eased that electricity throttle control forward, increasing the supply of voltage to the *Goddess'* veins of Skyrock and thus increasing the attack plane's altitude.

Centered in the roof of the cockpit was a raised turret on a platform, devoid of its own guns. It was from this turret's seat that Esteban Villalobos was controlling the giant craft's weapons remotely, and from where he would be able to single-handedly unleash a barrage upon Templo Del Sol's unsuspecting populace.

Storm stepped around the corner and into the cockpit, thrusting his pistol toward the gunnery station. "Take your hands off those controls, Villalobos." His voice was steady and firm.

Stunned, the dapper guerrilla looked down from his seat and saw the steely determination in Storm's eyes, the unwavering barrel of the Mauser pointed toward his heart. He released the control levers, the now uncontrolled guns falling silent behind the noise of the engine. He glared at Storm. "At last I meet you as myself, *señor*, and with no mask between us. I should have just killed you and your men myself in that police station. It would have certainly saved me from all this trouble."

"Get down from that turret." Storm jerked the barrel of his pistol downward, and Esteban followed his command. He slowly climbed down the steel ladder to the cockpit floor below and put his hands up. The pilot, meanwhile, had craned his neck over his shoulder when Storm had first spoken; he watched the two men, mute and goggle-eyed.

"You keep flying the plane," Storm snapped to the pilot. "We're turning around and heading back, aren't we Esteban?" He smiled at the corner of his mouth and felt a momentary tingle of triumph, until his captive's face seemed to twitch ever so slightly and he suddenly remembered…

…Jorge Villalobos.

The more brutish of the two brothers had snuck up behind Storm silently as he had neared the cockpit. He struck now, thrusting his thick arms forward and clamping them around Storm's chest from behind like an iron vice. Arms pinned and caught in the crushing bear-hug, Storm felt himself being squeezed out of his breath and being lifted bodily off of the floor, dropping his pistol involuntarily from his numbing fingers. He had to escape Jorge's beastly grip, and fast.

Storm rammed the back of his head into Jorge's nose. The sudden blow stunned the assailant momentarily and he loosened his grip only slightly, but it was enough for his quarry. Storm's hands dropped behind his body and he jabbed rigid fingers into twin pressure points on Jorge's hips. The effect was instantaneous: Jorge's legs sagged weakly as he dropped to the cockpit floor. Storm spun and kicked him hard in the gut, and Jorge let out a howl of sudden pain. Esteban, meanwhile, had lunged for Storm's dropped Mauser and snatched it up. Storm caught Esteban's dive in his peripheral vision, however, and rolled to the opposite corner of the cockpit. Esteban hastily aimed and shot into the space that Storm had just occupied and the bullet struck a blank wall and ricocheted.

Jorge had recovered and drew one of his own pistols and rose from the floor; he aimed the revolver toward Storm's new position, but his target recognized the new threat in a split second. Crouching, Storm's hand flashed to his back, where a knife was sheathed between his shoulder-blades in his utility harness. His hand snapped forward and a flashing glint of steel, like a miniature lightning bolt, sped between them. The knife was suddenly embedded in Jorge's wrist and he grunted in pain as he dropped his revolver.

The plane suddenly canted sharply to one side for a moment. The three men turned to look at the pilot. He sat sagging forward in his seat, a ragged hole from Esteban's ricocheted shot in the back of his head. From the pilot's lips, a scarlet river poured out onto the controls. He was dead.

Furious at the dying of his maniacal dream, Esteban gave an enraged yell and began firing the Mauser at Storm, but his target was already moving, leaping across the cockpit toward him. He tackled the warlord, sending him sprawling backward while the Mauser was knocked from his hand. The gun slid across the floor, out of the reach of either man.

Gripped as his own sickening fear of flying intensified, Jorge rose from his crouch and raced to the cockpit's emergency hatch. The plane was pilot-less, careening through the valley with two men struggling to kill each other inside…it was a sure recipe for disaster. The brutish yet cowardly Jorge cared nothing for the dream he had shared of domination now, cared nothing for the brother with whom he had shared that dream. All that mattered to him now was the frantic, primal urge to get away from the accursed super-plane before it crashed. He yanked the emergency exit door's lever and the panel flew open, wind suddenly shrieking into the *Goddess of Death's* interior. He leaped out into space. As soon as he was out the door he realized that the altitude of the craft was dangerously low now to the trees and he began to claw furiously at the ripcord of his parachute. A wall of green foliage was rushing up to meet him, but his blood-slicked hands finally found the pull-ring and he yanked it. The blossoming silken shroud opened above him and snapped him upward violently. He floated downward, relieved that he'd had the foresight to strap into a 'chute, toward the onrushing jungle canopy below…

Skids, following the strange plane in the *Witch*, had been watching the other craft's erratic actions intently as his concern rose. When he saw the bloom of a parachute he became hopeful, but only until he got a closer look and saw the stocky body of Jorge Villalobos beneath it. He floated, like ragweed in the wind, down toward the jungle. Skids decided to circle the warlord's landing spot to fix it in his memory before resuming his chase.

As he neared he could see the white silk of the parachute had become tangled in the trees and below it hung Jorge Villalobos, his boots dangling just a few feet from the ground. Skids had a brief worry that the warlord would escape but it was dashed suddenly as he caught a glimpse of several large grey shadows moving swiftly through the undergrowth toward Jorge…

Satisfied at the ironic and natural justice taking place below, Skids broke from his circle and sped again toward the *Goddess of Death* weaving in the sky in the distance.

Jorge Villalobos had bailed out far too low to the ground. His fall hadn't been slowed very much before he hit the trees of the jungle, and in his plummet through the branches he had felt a nauseating snap in his left forearm. From his broken skin, a spear of white splintered bone had broken through. Both arms were now useless and running with blood, but he congratulated himself on being alive and he laughed as he dangled not far from the ground. He would find a way to get down; he would hide somewhere and find a doctor who could help him and keep quiet about it. Jorge Villalobos would live to fight again. Who knew? Perhaps he would start a new empire by himself...

A sudden movement caught his eye. He looked up from the ground below him and met the gaze of a wolf. He realized that he wasn't entirely alone. He was surrounded by a trio of haggard, ghostly-looking wolves...

...They were his wolves.

They sniffed the air and licked their curling lips, and they began to step closer to where he hung helplessly.

Oh, God, Jorge thought feverishly, the blood. They can smell my blood.

He fumbled with his ruined arms at his second pistol, but his fingers were numb and bloody and in agony, and they slipped again and again from the leather holster empty. Jorge, the ugly, battle-hardened and blood-thirsty warlord, began to weep.

There was a growl and a grey blur, then another; another. The starving wolves hit him like sledgehammers, clawing and biting his flesh with a savage chorus of snarls. Jorge's sobs became screams, and flocks of panicked birds fled at the sound as it echoed through the jungle.

From that moment onward, Jorge's wolves would never be hungry ever again.

Above the valley. The *Goddess of Death* was pitching wildly, its multi-directional engines screaming in protest at the lack of control. Inside the cockpit, Storm and Esteban found themselves locked in hand-to-hand combat. All around them, the delicate electronics were popping with sparks, overloading and failing, and a fire alarm bell had begun claninging madly. The copilot's seat had caught fire and the cockpit was filling with smoke; it trailed out of the open emergency hatch like a streamer of grey behind the plane.

The Mauser had slid from out from its hiding place and across the floor toward the combatants, and Esteban was straining to reach it. Storm's fingers were locked around his wrists, but Esteban's feet had found leverage against a console and his fingers inched closer as he pushed.

Storm drove his knee into the other man's solar plexus, driving the air from Esteban's lungs in a resounding "whoosh" of sound. In raising his leg, however, he lost his balance and the two men tumbled across the floor to the other side of the cockpit.

Esteban snaked a wrist free of Storm's grasp and drove a staggering blow to his foe's chin. Stunned momentarily, Storm loosened his grip. Esteban crawled hurriedly toward the gun. Storm had recovered quickly and gripped Esteban's ankle in a vise-like fist. Roaring with anger, Esteban kicked his other leg out, colliding with Storm's nose in a bloody spray. The grip never loosened, however, and Storm pulled the warlord back toward him by the leg. When it was within reach, Storm gripped Esteban's collar with his right hand and with his left fist he sledged at his opponent's face again and again. His punches connected with explosive force, eventually driving the consciousness from Esteban.

Storm stood up bloody and disheveled, and turned toward the controls. The craft pitched, nearly knocking Storm from his feet. Ahead in the distance he could see the faint beginnings of civilization and knew it was going to crash into the huts and houses there. He looked around the cockpit, anger in his eyes. He burned then, suddenly filled with unutterable rage at the *Goddess of Death* and its makers. He had to destroy it right away, to remove it from the earth completely before it cause any more chaos.

He gripped the electrical throttle-lever, bringing the craft low over the river below, and when the plane was low enough Storm kicked the electrical throttle to its full stops, then kicked again. He kicked a third time as the craft started to shoot upward like a rocket, and he kept kicking. His brain was filled with images of Katherine Tolliver's starved frame, of the hordes of slaves that had been used and discarded in the construction of the super-plane, of the intended destruction of Templo Del Sol and enslavement of La Isla de Sangre, of the human lives taken in the lawless battle between evil men.

With a final savage kick the throttle-like lever broke off, locking the Skyrock-infused lift-system into overdrive. The plane pitched and threatened to throw Storm off his feet, and he knew that he had to act fast. He turned away and raced through the shuddering and erratically rising craft's cockpit to the open emergency exit hatch. He leaped out into the open air...

Esteban awoke as the plane's nose pitched up. He found himself sliding toward the back of the plane as the floor tilted, but not before he glimpsed Clifton Storm as he jumped from the emergency hatch. Esteban clawed his way back across the tilted floor toward the cockpit but he knew that by the time he reached it that he would be too late. The Skyrock was now supersaturated with electricity now; the plane was shuddering and groaning under the effects of the broken anti-gravity mechanisms. It rose faster and faster and he knew that it would never stop. Even if he could make it to the hatch he knew that it would be hopeless: by then the ground would be too far away for him to jump without a parachute, and by the time he could find and strap on a 'chute the *Goddess of Death* would be in the stratosphere. Breathing would soon be impossible.

Resigned to his fate, Esteban Villalobos looked down and watched from the nearest window as the Isle of Blood spun and receded below.

When Storm had leaped from the emergency hatch he instantly wished he had handled things differently. Perhaps he should simply have tried to crash the plane into the jungle. Flying it was probably out of the question, but maybe a different approach would have worked better. Maybe he could have managed to bring it down before it reached the edge of the city beyond… It made no difference now: the craft was plunging helplessly upward while he was heading in the opposite direction. The river below was speeding up to meet him.

Storm twisted his body, pointing his feet toward the water. He hoped at least this way that if he broke any bones when he struck the water it would be his legs only and not his skull. He stiffened, bracing for impact.

He hit the water, which seemed suddenly like a solid wall of dark glass, and he blacked out. His next conscious moment found him clawing his way to the sunlight-dappled surface of the river. His nerves sang with pain but he was alive.

His head broke the surface, and he shook the water from his eyes and gazed upward. Above, the broken and smoking *Goddess of Death* continued its pinwheel into the sky. It grew smaller, receding, becoming a violet star in the deep blue heavens above.

Storm managed to swim to the riverbank and there he lay exhausted, watching the shrinking spot in the early evening sky. He gradually became aware that Skids was circling in the *Witch* above him. Storm smiled weakly and gratefully, and raised his hand in a wave toward his comrade.

CHAPTER 23: THE HOUSE OF WOLVES FALLS

ack at the Villalobos compound, a series of paddy wagons had arrived and were being loaded to the brim with the surrendered guerrilla soldiers. Police agents were raiding the offices and private quarters of the Villalobos Brothers: they were seeking (and were finding) the proof that would indict crooked police from all over La Isla de Sangre. The destroyed armory was a smoldering wreck, but agents were going over it with as much scrutiny as possible in seeking clues there as well.

"We are hoping to find information that will lead us to a black-market arms dealer whom we've heard has been expanding his operations in this area," Anando Del Rio was telling Clifton Storm, who had been looked after by a medic and had changed into dry clothes; he was now smoking one of his custom-blended cigars. It was a little thing Storm did at the completion of a job, a tiny victory celebration. The scent of hazelnut wafted from the cigar on the breeze, which was surprisingly cool and felt good after the harsh events of the day's adventure.

"Hopefully, there'll be enough evidence to answer some of those burning questions," Storm said.

"Believe me," Del Rio replied, "what you've done here has helped us tremendously. Our entire nation is in your debt, Mr. Storm."

"As am I," chimed in J. Gordon Tolliver. He and Katherine had walked up to the pair during their discussion. Along with the father and daughter pair was Willy, Brock, and Skids. "I cannot thank you enough, Mr. Storm.

My daughter is safe now, and I'm going to donate a huge portion of my earnings from White Heron to the slaves and their families. It's the very least I can do."

"And that was his idea, not mine," said Kate flashing a tired but beaming smile. "Thank you Mr. Storm; I owe you and your men my life. I think my father has learned his lesson through all this, too. He and I have a lot to discuss about things that happened here, but it's nothing that we can't sort out now." She hugged her father closer.

"Now, as long as we're talking about discussing things and answering questions," Willy spoke up to Storm, "how about you answer some of our own?"

"Starting with how you managed your little resurrection," Skids said.

"Well, it's a long story, but I'll start at the beginning" began Storm, "I was always suspicious of Richard Stein, right from the moment we entered his house in Templo Del Sol." He puffed on his cigar. "For a man whose fiancé had been kidnapped and was in danger, I noticed that nothing of her existence showed up in his house. There were pictures everywhere, showing career highlights, his social life, rich and famous people he'd rubbed shoulders with... but not a single photo of Kate. I hope you don't mind me discussing this, Ms. Tolliver."

"Not at all," said the teacher. "Richard is part of the past now. I won't look back at him with any fondness."

"But those pictures," suggested Brock, "they could have been elsewhere, maybe in another room," suggested Brock.

"You're exactly right," said Storm, "which is why I just filed it away as just a minor fact." He tapped his forehead. "The second tip-off was how he defended the man we knew then as Panza, even though we'd been involved in a set-up and he was a suspect, but then that could've been just pig-headed loyalty on Stein's part." He took another puff on the cigar. "The biggest tips, though, were yet to come.

"First, there was the damaged engine on the *Seeing Red*. The cops at the airfield were outfitted with small pistols: .38 revolvers. The bullet-hole in the engine was of a bigger caliber, something like a .45... the kind that Stein carried."

Storm reached up to the bandages on his head, touching them gently. "Of course, the final clincher for me- and this was real proof- was the recording I found on the *Seeing Red*'s transmission logger."

Willy, Skids, and Brock grinned knowingly, while Del Rio and the Tollivers looked on, puzzled.

Storm explained: "Each one of our planes have a device of my own invention installed and attached to the radio set. The transmission logger is a device that keeps records of all radio communications, both sent and received. Each transmission is recorded electronically along with information regarding the frequencies that were used for them and compass readings of the plane's location at the time the transmissions are made. I hope that one day this kind of device will be installed in all aircraft, so that their communications can be studied should something go wrong and the plane crash.

"Anyway, last night, when Stein was preparing to bed down, he had gone into the *Seeing Red* to get his things. While he was inside, he made a call to the Villalobos Brothers using the radio, never once realizing it was being recorded.

"I snuck into the plane after everyone was asleep and listened to the call. Knowing we would trust him he would take us by surprise and would deliver us as his hostages to the Villalobos compound. The way I figured it, somebody would have to follow them and blow the whistle on their base's location; otherwise nobody would know where we were. Del Rio knew approximately where we were, but he couldn't know the exact location without someone telling him.

"My plan was elaborate and dangerous and not just a bit stupid, but it worked," he continued. "I had to separate myself from the group. I wanted Richard Stein to think that I was dead. We didn't get along, even superficially, and I knew he'd jump at the first chance to shoot me no matter what the Villalobos Brothers wanted him to do. And so I snuck into the tent he shared with Mr. Tolliver and swapped his pistol's ammo with signal caps in preparation for the next day."

"Signal caps?" asked Katherine Tolliver.

"Noisemaker shells," Willy explained. "We use them to signal our location to each other in the field. There's no bullet, but it sounds like a regular gun-shot… maybe louder."

Storm nodded in agreement. "I had my spot all picked out," he said. "I made sure that when the time came I was standing on an overhang on the lip of the valley, and on the underside of that were some vine-like roots. When Stein 'shot' me, I fell and grabbed onto those vines and hid beneath the overhang. From his viewpoint, Stein couldn't see me when he looked down."

"That was all a hell of a far-fetched gamble, Cliff," said Brock. "How'd you know this would all work?"

"I didn't," smiled Storm. "It was a long shot but it was my only idea besides a confrontation and interrogation, and I knew that wouldn't work because of Stein's famously stubborn personality. He wouldn't talk and rat on the Villalobos Brothers… and in the end they betrayed him, the man who helped them come close to realizing their dream of conquest.

"After Stein assumed I was dead and led you guys away from the camp, I called Del Rio from the radio on board the *Seeing Red* and had him ready as many trustworthy police members as possible. After that I managed to follow and pick up your trail through the jungle and to the compound and was able to sneak inside myself. I managed to disguise myself enough to blend in without being too conspicuous, and I was able to use one of their radios to call Del Rio again and gave him the base's location. Then I scrounged up some weapons that I was able to sneak from the Villalobos Brother's armory and concealed them.

"The bombs in the armory," he continued, "were both a distraction and a signal to the coming strike-force… I'm just sorry they went off at the last second like they did." Storm grinned. "There's nothing like a split-second rescue for high-dramatics, even though I wasn't aiming for that, and I thought for a minute or two before they went off that I would have to come up with an alternate plan, and fast.

"After the bombs went off it was just a matter of hiding and, if necessary, holding them off until the cavalry showed up… which of course is where that stash of their weapons that I managed to hide earlier came into play."

"Well," Tolliver said after a moment, "this seems like it irons out the mysteries and some of La Isla de Sangre's problems. The Villalobos Brothers destroyed their competition themselves, and then you and the police stopped the Villalobos Brothers."

"Loose ends, all tied up," said Katherine Tolliver. Then she noticed Rosa being led by a medic from where she had been hiding across the compound. "Well," she said sadly, "maybe not all the loose ends." The group followed her gaze to the vacant-eyed girl in the distance.

"*Dios mio*," Del Rio breathed, and broke from the group and into a run toward Rosa.

"What…?" exclaimed Kate.

"That final loose end is tying itself up," said Storm, puffing on his cigar and smiling.

Rosa looked up, her slack face suddenly springing to life. Her eyes were suddenly alive and sparkling with tears of joy, and all the pain and horror she'd endured seemed to melt and slough off. "Papa!" she shouted, running toward Del Rio, and they embraced.

As the second father-daughter reunion of the day unfolded before Storm and his men, he looked around, reflecting on the events.

A mission to save a single life had ended with an entire nation freed from the tyranny of guerrillas. Kidnapped and mistreated people, the slaves of Villalobos, were freed and families had been mended. As he stood there with his friends, the man whom the world called "Challenger" remembered a decision he had made on a desolate mountain a long time ago- a decision to help the innocent and punish the guilty- and he knew that it was never going to be enough for him. The bad things were never going to stop happening to good people, and he would never stop doing what he could to help those people. It was going to be an uphill and never ending battle, a war that he knew he could never truly win.

But for the moment, Clifton Storm and his men were happy with what they had done on La Isla de Sangre, and that was enough for them.

EPILOGUE
&
COMING ATTRACTIONS...

t was Sunday morning. In the distance the waves were crashing lazily on the beach beyond the fence at the MARDL compound, and a squadron of seagulls wheeled and cried in the sky above the whitecaps out in Biscayne Bay. Other than these sounds most of the compound was quiet. It was a day of rest for the Miami Aerodrome Research and Development Labs, and all the personnel- scientists, engineers, staff and troubleshooters- were off work and ensconced in their private lives away from the area.

The network of buildings was empty... empty of all the personnel but one.

In the main hangar, Clifton Storm sat working beneath the wing of a small plane, a Percival Gull monoplane named *Little Linda* that was suspended from the ceiling by chains. There had been some problems with the port landing gear and he was now working busily on the assembly. In the corner, Buddy the terrier sat contentedly chewing a rawhide strip, his large eyes half-closed in the lazy enjoyment of the chew-toy. On the radio at a nearby shelf Ethel Waters sang "Stormy Weather," a melancholy song that floated up to echo in ghostly tones among the rafters of the hangar.

As he worked, Storm's eye was caught by a pair of white MARDL coveralls hanging in the corner much like the ones that he was wearing. The hanging work-outfit had yet to be washed, and it was covered with streaks of red: traces of the Isle of Blood's scarlet clay that seemed to permeate everything they had brought back with them from their adventure. It had been several days since they had returned to Florida and they were still finding the stuff everywhere (especially Skids and Brock, who had the same idea for a prank and had hid shovelfuls of the clay in each other's luggage).

Storm smiled as he reflected on their experiences in La Isla de Sangre. Overall he considered it a job well done, but the poverty of the island's people still affected him. Their condition was going to be slow to overcome, and he regretted not being able to help them more. It was at times like this that he wished he had unlimited wealth; if he did, he would gladly give continued assistance to anyone in the world who was in need, but that was just a pipe dream. He was extremely wealthy, but even his considerable riches had limitations.

A gust of wind blew lazily into the hangar, and Storm's mind drew farther back, before the Isle of Blood case and to the incident with the *Goliath* airship. There were still unanswered mysteries that surrounded that case. The identity of the hijackers, for example, had never been made public and they had never been revealed to Storm either. He had been interviewed and debriefed by members of the State Department shortly after the incident, and he had told them all he knew from his life-saving actions. The hijackers had been foreign and had spoken a language that had been extremely similar to Estonian. Their uniforms had been grey and featureless, devoid of any kind of decorations or flags to denote their country. There had been two separate units at work within the *Goliath*; one had operated within the areas where guns couldn't be fired onboard, the other within the sealed passenger areas. The only insignia the units wore had been zodiacal symbols: the highly skilled archers that he had encountered among the airship's gas-bags had worn the symbol of Sagittarius, while the more plentiful and gun-carrying foot soldiers in the hydrogen-free areas had carried the Gemini insignia upon their uniforms. They had all exhibited the signs of fanaticism in their behavior, and Storm had no doubt that they were capable of murder on a grand scale if they had desired to carry such an act out. They had been highly skilled and dangerous men, but that was where his knowledge of those mysterious enemies had ended. After his interview, the government men had simply nodded at him. "Thank you," they said. "We'll be in touch."

That was the last he'd heard from them. It was now early November. Nearly two months had passed without notice or comment or any word at all from the G-Men, and Storm was beginning to wonder if anything more would be heard about the incident or the hijackers at all...

Ethel Waters' voice disappeared suddenly with a click. Someone had shut off the radio.

Without the warm tones from the radio, the sudden silence was like a vacuum, and even the soft sounds of the wind and waves on the bay seemed rapidly hushed. Buddy stopped his chewing and his ears stood up straight, and Storm looked at the dog as he stared past the plane and into the depths of the hangar. Buddy growled, low and concerned and Storm stood up slowly. He held a heavy wrench in his left hand and picked up a screwdriver in his right.

Looking past the wing of the Percival, the recesses of the hangar looked drenched in shadow, despite the sun streaming though the high windows that spottily illuminated the floor. Buddy had gotten up from his corner, his rawhide strip forgotten. He stood next to his master and growled again, and someone moved in the shadows. No one was scheduled to be at the compound beside Storm, who lived there, and Buddy never growled at anyone on the MARDL staff. The dog barked a challenge to the figure in the shadows.

"Come on out, friend," Storm called without fear but ready to fight if need be. "This is private property, and you'd better have a damned good reason to be here."

The man in the shadows stepped forward into the light, and Storm's eyes narrowed. The visitor was a blond man with a blandly handsome face and a slight half-smile pulling up one corner of his mouth. His suit and hat were jet-black and his tie was a hideous lime-green color; all of his clothing looked so immaculately and severely pressed that it appeared almost hard. The man reached into his coat pocket and Storm tensed for action, primed to take action if necessary. But instead of rapidly drawing a weapon, the mystery visitor drew a small leather case from his coat and flicked it open. Identification papers met Storm's eye along with an unusual gold badge.

"Clifton Storm," he addressed the adventurer with a firm voice, "my name's Matheson. Special Agent Jim Matheson of the United States global-threat task-force. Our more common name for the task-force is The Eye." He started to put the leather wallet away, but Storm stepped toward him and reached for it.

"If I may," he said to Matheson, and the agent handed it to him. "In my business, one can't be too careful," he explained as he opened the case. Matheson smiled.

"It works the same way in my line of work. Go ahead."

Storm closely examined the paperwork and identification forms in the wallet. Although Matheson's group was unheard of by Storm, the ID and paperwork looked authentic and had several seals and signatures of some very highly-placed government officials. The badge was unusual too. Against the shield shape of the golden badge was a series of black and royal-blue abstract lines and shapes and after a moment of scrutiny the design revealed itself as an art-deco stylized depiction of a staring eyeball. "The Eye, huh?" he said as he handed the case back to Matheson. "I can't say I've ever heard of it."

"That means we're doing our job," the agent replied with a slight chuckle. He put the case away.

"So what can I do for you, Agent Matheson?" Storm asked as he folded his arms and leaned back against a work bench. Buddy, convinced there was not going to be a need to protect his master, trotted back to the corner and renewed chewing his toy. He kept his eyes on the newcomer, however, just in case he was needed.

"Well, it's more of a case of what we can do for each other, Mr. Storm." Matheson shoved his hands in his trouser pockets and gazed around the hangar. "This is a most impressive set-up you have here. It's really something."

Storm wasn't sure if the government man was truly admiring his work or simply patronizing him. "Alright, then. What can we do for each other, Agent Matheson? Why are you here?"

The agent turned back toward Storm. "Do you remember that incident not too long ago with the airship *Goliath*?" Storm nodded, considering the irony that he himself had just been thinking about it. "As you may recall," Matheson went on, "we were having a pretty hard time getting any information out of that team of hijackers that you neutralized. No matter how much interrogation we tried or what methods we used, they kept their mouth shut. Then, after two days of questioning the situation was made all the more aggravating when the men were found dead in their cells."

Storm raised an eyebrow. "Suicide?"

"Well, yes and no... and maybe," Matheson said, pushing his fedora back on his head. "When we found them, they all had broken necks but they hadn't hung themselves. Nor did it seem that they did it to each other, as the positions of the bodies were all too far away from each other. There were no fingerprints on the corpses to show that any outside party had done it, but that could've been hidden by gloves of course... until we discovered no bruising that would have been made at another's hand. Either there was another man or group of men who snuck in the cells, broke their necks with some kind of secret method and left without a trace; or..." he paused to step outside the hangar door and light a cigarette, "or they broke their own necks."

"Is that possible?" Storm asked.

"Well, you tell me. You're the mystery man, traveling from Tibet to Timbuktu looking for adventure and all that. Ever seen anything like it?"

Storm considered for a moment. "Certain far-eastern disciplines teach complete body control and mastery. Perhaps there's some kind of suicide maneuver taught in one of those kinds of martial arts or a rogue faction of such, but if there is I've never heard of it."

"Well, regardless of how it happened, it *has* happened and our trail has gone pretty cold in one hell of a hurry. Or at least it did, until we got some leads from a deep-cover agent of ours overseas."

Storm stepped out of the hangar and into the sunlight with Matheson, his curiosity piqued. "So, who were they? Where were they from?"

"I'm sorry, Storm. We can't give out that information to anybody, not even to you. Not yet, anyway. And that's why I'm here.

"See, what you have here in Miami, Mr. Storm," he continued to explain, "is basically a combination of private detective agency and non-profit vigilante group. Sure, you've got a well known aeronautics and design laboratory, and there's nothing wrong with that. But that other side to your organization, your 'troubleshooters'... there's a legal mess waiting to happen. As noble as your intentions may be, you will need sanctioning if you want to continue your crusade without interference. And that's where we come in."

"I'm afraid I don't follow you," Storm said. It wasn't entirely true. He was beginning to feel as though he was about to be blackmailed or something else sinister was going on. He was eager to cut to the chase.

"We- me, The Eye, the entire U.S. government- want to offer you immunity and protection against any such action," Matheson told him. "The freedom to continue your fine work here is all yours... if you agree to help us."

Clifton Storm was a patriot. He believed in what he was doing because it kept innocent people- and his country- free from tyrants and criminals. He was prepared to assist. "How can I help, Agent Matheson?"

The G-man flashed his smirk again. "There are certain cases that the U.S. government needs to be in on, but we can't. There are places that need to be visited, actions that need to be completed and so forth that we simply can't be involved with publicly. Shaky politics keep us tied from these actions officially and so we need an outside agent. We need someone with resources, skills, an affinity for such an adventure... we need someone with talent."

"So you're saying you need someone like me," Storm said slowly, considering every word that was said and what Matheson was offering him.

"Exactly," the agent nodded back. "We need somebody we can count on, but who is a free agent. We need somebody who can get things done with a minimum of our assistance because if that agent was caught... well, I'm not going to lie to you. If you were caught we would publicly deny your involvement with us and we'd cut all our ties with you. It is dangerous work, and it stinks that we can't help you if the chips are down... but damn it, Storm, we need you."

Storm looked around the compound. It was his life's ambition, his all-consuming dream to make the world better. Some called it Quixotic, others claimed it wouldn't be enough... but others had been helped by him: they were proof that what he and MARDL were doing was something good, something that the world sorely needed. And others still were counting on him for help in the future. Somewhere out there were others who would need him: the oppressed and the beaten down and the hopeless. How could he let them down? He would need assurance that his dream lived and thrived, and in helping the government in their missions he would be helping his country in turn, maybe even helping the world. It was an extension of his dream, and the cynical side of his nature finally gave way to the side that was the idealist in him. But he had to make sure things were on the level...

"Okay, I'm in, Matheson. But first, I have some demands."

The agent looked taken back, but replied. "If they're within reason, then you can have your demands."

"They're within reason to me," Storm said. "First: when I become involved I want full disclosure... I need to know exactly what I'm dealing with, all the details."

"That's reasonable," Matheson said, nodding. "What else?"

"Second," Storm continued, "my people become involved if I need them, and they get full disclosure too."

Matheson drew air in between his teeth. "That one's touchy. We're talking about matters of national security here."

"Yes, and we're also talking about the safety of my crew. I won't lead them blindly into hell without telling them where we're going."

The agent thought this over for a moment. "Okay, you can tell them… but only those involved in a particular case. This information is only given out on a need-to-know basis, and they'll be the only ones that need to know."

Storm nodded. "Alright, that's fair enough. Third and lastly: I want the right to deny any jobs that are offered to me. If I smell even a hint of fishiness, I'm not taking on anything."

Matheson looked at him steadily. "You can turn down our offers if you want to, yes. But be aware that by doing so you and your agency here will be cast in a different light. The more of our jobs that you turn down, the less assistance we can give in assuring that you steer clear of red tape."

"I'm prepared for that." Storm's gaze was icy and confident.

Matheson looked out to the waters of the bay. After a moment he looked back at the adventurer and said, "You've got your deals, Mr. Storm. Don't think I would have been so lenient in our negotiations with you if we didn't need your proven skills as much as we do, though."

Storm smiled. "I'm sorry if I put up a fight, but I'm trying to keep everyone's best interests in mind." He wiped his greasy hand on his coveralls and offered it to Matheson, who smiled back and shook it firmly.

"We're glad to have you aboard, Storm. Your country is grateful for all your help."

Storm shrugged and turned back to the hangar. "I'm just doing the right thing… that's all I ever try to do," he said over his shoulder as he walked back to the Percival Gull. "Now, is there anything you can tell me about what you've learned about those hijackers?"

"Not yet," Matheson said from the hangar doorway. "That's that 'need-to-know' information that you and I just talked about. But should your help be needed, you'll get to know everything that we do."

Storm looked back at him for a moment, wondering how much he would ever know about the *Goliath* incident if he wasn't involved in it again. "Alright then, I expected as much." He turned back toward the plane. "Do you have a business card, Matheson, some way I can get back in touch with you?"

"No. We'll contact you if needed," he said back to Storm. "And we'll also know if you need us. Remember, Storm: the Eye is always watching."

Storm smiled at the serial-like dramatics, and turned to say as much to Matheson but stopped, his mouth hanging open. The G man was no longer at the doorway.

He stepped over to the door and out into the sunlit grass outside, Buddy trotting eagerly at his heels. The calm Sunday morning surrounded the man and his dog, but there was no one else in sight. Special Agent Jim Matheson had disappeared without a trace, completely and ghost-like.

Storm looked down at Buddy, who looked back up and wagged his stubby little tail, his panting face like an open-mouthed grin.

"Wow... that guy's good," Storm said to the dog, and the two turned back to walk toward the cavernous hangar.

THE END

ABOUT OUR CREATORS:

ichael Wm. Kaluta was born in Guatemala to U.S. citizens. He studied at the Richmond Professional Institute (now Virginia Commonwealth University). Michael is probably best known for his work on the comic book series *Starstruck* and *The Shadow*.

Kaluta's early work included Charlton Comics *Flash Gordon* and an adaptation of Edgar Rice Burroughs's *Venus* novels for DC. Kaluta's influences and style are drawn from pulp illustrations of the 1930s and the turn of the century poster work of Alphonse Mucha rather than the silver age comics of the 1960s. Associated during the 1970s with Bernie Wrightson and Jeffrey Jones he also contributed illustrations to Ted White's *Fantastic* and *Amazing*. He co-created *Eve*, the horror host turned *The Sandman* supporting character.

Kaluta was one of the four comic book artists/fine illustrators/painters who formed the artists' commune The Studio in a loft in Manhattan's Chelsea district from 1975 to 1979 with Barry Windsor-Smith, Jeffrey Jones, and Bernie Wrightson. Aside from many comic books and covers, Kaluta has done a wide variety of book illustrations.

In 1984, he not only drew the illustrations for but directed the music video of The Alan Parsons Project song *Don't Answer Me,* which became one of the most requested videos of the year on cable video channel *MTV*.

Among music fans, Kaluta is known as the artist for the cover of Glenn Danzig's instrumental album *Black Aria* and for the interior illustration of Danzig's fourth album, the latter of which appeared in 1994 and 1995 as a pendant sold at Danzig concerts, and on Danzig T-shirts and sweaters produced in the same period. Kaluta also created the CD covers and interior booklet illustrations for *Nativity in Black I* and *II*, tribute albums to the music of Black Sabbath.

Kaluta has also worked for role-playing game companies such as

White Wolf. He has done artwork for collectible card games companies, including a comic book for Wizards of the Coast's *Magic: The Gathering* and illustrating cards on Last Unicorn Games' *Heresy: Kingdom Come*.

His work has won him a good deal of recognition, including the Shazam Award for Outstanding New Talent in 1971 and the 2003 Spectrum Grandmaster Award.

Don Gates is a native of Florida, something of a rarity in the Sunshine State. Born in 1974, he has worked for a toy store and a bakery, worked in a trophy shop and with the developmentally disabled, and has worked customer service from magazine subscriptions to home-phone service. He is married to a loving and feisty wife and the pair have seven "children": 2 dogs, 3 cats. Gates recently moved to Canada and is learning to deal with the weather, which is often a far cry from that of Florida. *The Isle of Blood* is Gates' first novel, and was followed up in 2014 with the second novel in the Challenger Storm series, *The Curse of Poseidon*.

DEATH BENEATH THE WAVES

When several cargo ships begin disappearing on the waters of the Aegean Sea rumors begin to spread about black-armored demons rising up out of the deep. For Challenger Storm and his MARDL team, these events hold no particular interest until one of Storm's troubleshooters, Diana St.Clair, informs him that her former lover, and one-time MARDL scientist, Herbert Chambers is among the missing.

Later, a freakish wave wipes out a small Greek fishing village leaving only a handful of survivors. Is it possible someone has learned how to control the seas to do their bidding? When Storm and his companions arrive at a mid-ocean refueling station, they are attacked by saboteurs wielding bizarre rifles that fire sea-water.

Who is the mysterious figure calling himself Poseidon and what is the secret of his ability to create monstrous tidal waves? Can Challenger Storm find his underwater base in time to stop this mad genius before he rains down more watery destruction upon unsuspecting coastal populations? Is mankind doomed to be ruled by a new King of the Seas?

Here is high-octane pulp adventure on…and below the waves!

PULP FICTION FOR A NEW GENERATION!

FOR AVAILABILITY CHECK: AIRSHIP27HANGAR.COM

SET SAIL FOR ADVENTURE

The greatest seafaring adventurer of all time returns to the high seas, *Sinbad the Sailor!*

Born of countless legends and myths, this fearless rogue sets sail across the seven seas aboard his ship, the Blue Nymph, accompanied by an international crew of colorful, larger-than-life characters. Chief among these are the irascible Omar, a veteran seamen and trusted first mate, the blond Viking giant, Ralf Gunarson, the sophisticated archer from Gaul, Henri Delacrois and the mysterious, lovely and deadly female samurai, Tishimi Osara. All of them banded together to follow their famous captain on perilous new voyages across the world's oceans.

So pack up your you traveling bags, bid ado to your loved ones and get ready to sail with the tide as Sinbad El Ari takes the tiller and the Blue Nymph sets sails once more; its destination worlds of wonder, mystery and high adventure.